T0129818

OTTER TAIL REVIEW,
VOLUME THREE

OTTER TAIL REVIEW, VOLUME THREE

Tim Rundquist, Editor

iUniverse, Inc.
New York   Bloomington

Copyright © 2009 by Tim Rundquist, Editor

All rights reserved. No part of this book may be used or reproduced by any means, graphic, electronic, or mechanical, including photocopying, recording, taping or by any information storage retrieval system without the written permission of the publisher except in the case of brief quotations embodied in critical articles and reviews.

iUniverse books may be ordered through booksellers or by contacting:

iUniverse
1663 Liberty Drive
Bloomington, IN 47403
www.iuniverse.com
1-800-Authors (1-800-288-4677)

Because of the dynamic nature of the Internet, any Web addresses or links contained in this book may have changed since publication and may no longer be valid. The views expressed in this work are solely those of the author and do not necessarily reflect the views of the publisher, and the publisher hereby disclaims any responsibility for them.

ISBN: 978-1-4401-7832-0 (sc)
ISBN: 978-1-4401-7833-7 (ebook)

Printed in the United States of America

iUniverse rev. date: 10/20/2009

Contents

PART TWO

PART THREE

PART FOUR

Foreword

Ever since graduating from a car seat, my daughter Rosemary has been my faithful co-pilot on a myriad of adventures around Otter Tail County. Vintage county map (with the great old-fashioned hand lettering) across her lap, she will point to a spot and say "What's this place?" or "Daddy, I don't think we've been here before." After several years of such explorations (which I began at a similar age, with my own Dad), it's safe to say that she knows the back-roads of the county as well as almost anyone.

Rosemary even works on maps of her own. For example, the path between Fergus Falls and the family compound at Otter Tail and Walker lakes is so well-worn in her mind that she has established the route via a series of landmarks, faithfully rendered in crayon, Magic Marker and other media. In a nutshell, the "typical" journey goes something like this:

1. Pretty Log House, With Horses;
2. Jewett Lake (where the Jewett people live, like Grandma Robyn);
3. The Place Where Daddy Almost Hit a Deer (low, boggy, dense tamarack and spruce);
4. Chrissy's House;
5. Junky Tractors;
6. The Dirt Eskimos (large, rounded domes of construction sand and gravel);
7. Big Floody Spot (yet another site in the county where the rising water table is submerging roads);
8. Silly Animals (where llamas, peacocks, reindeer and other exotica are raised);
9. The Round Barn[1];

10. Twin Lakes (Go Twins!)
11. Amor Cemetery (hold breath while passing, otherwise you'll die); and finally
12. We're Almost To The Cabin![2]

Alternative routes, taken while further exploring or deliberately getting lost, have led us to the discovery of such wonders as the Water Street bridge (depicted on the cover of this volume), a second Round Barn (smaller than the first, but also red), and Mr. Boen's new windmill at Bluebird Gardens. The thrill of such new discoveries, combined with the adrenaline rush of spotting a pond full of swans, or nearly miring ourselves in early-spring mud on those back roads, is not to be underestimated.

And so, guided by maps, spontaneity and our own imaginations, we transform an otherwise routine drive, one that we do dozens of times per year, into a journey of significance, marked by the signposts that we have created together. The more literal members of our family just shake their heads— but Rosemary and I know where *all* of the important landmarks are.

Otter Tail County, physical and spiritual home of the Otter Tail Review, is positively littered with landmarks of all types. There are, of course, the natural landmarks, which I have referenced in prior Reviews and my own writing: examples include the north-shore "point" of Otter Tail Lake (where the "Indian Princess" of Volume Two stood, so many years ago), as well as the eponymous "tail of the otter" (a long, thin sandbar) that gave the lake and river their names. Man-made landmarks are plentiful as well: ranging from the architecturally significant (the Kirkbride Tower) to the historic (Phelps Mill) to the undeniably cheesy (the giant Chief Wenonga statue in Battle Lake).

Personal experiences and history, of course, provide conspicuous landmarks as well. Births and deaths, marriages, graduations and other milestones provide a means of navigation for making sense of our lives in retrospect. For example, it is very easy for me to break down my adult life in terms of pre-marriage, post-child, etc.; otherwise I may not be able to pinpoint when, exactly, I heeled a 30-foot sloop in the chilly waters of lake Superior while sailing with my cousin and her husband (it was the weekend before I proposed to Heather, right after we had finished smashing up some old bathroom tile), and those early-parenting days, in particular, would likely run together in a sleep-deprived blur.

A community, by which I mean any cohesive gathering of people, will observe landmarks as measured by time or particular events. Camp Nidaros, founded by my great-grandfather and five other Lutheran pastors seeking respite from their hard-working daily lives, celebrated its 100th anniversary in Summer 2009 (a few days prior to this writing), marked by a pot-luck at Phelps Mill (no Minnesota celebration is truly complete without hot dish), countless stories, and a volume of family histories and photographs spanning six generations. Fergus Falls, Minnesota, where I live, is defined in large part by the events of June 1919, when a cyclone destroyed a substantial portion of the city. During the height of storm season this past June, I could not help but flash back to 1919 when I saw those dark, greenish wall clouds approaching, and heard the sirens that would soon send my family and I to the basement. Rosemary's early life was marked by a huge windstorm out at the cabin, when she was five, which left an indelible impression of fallen trees and about twenty terrifying minutes in the back bedroom. That storm likely left its mark on everyone in the community who was affected by it.

All in all, landmarks can guide our way through what seems at first blush to be a featureless landscape— or the mundanity of our daily lives— but in fact is loaded with significance. The hope is that this book can show us some of those important landmarks, whether for the first time or in a new light.

A final note: two of the final written works of Bill Holm, one of the greatest writers Minnesota has ever produced (and certainly one of the tallest), bookend this volume. In February 2009, Bill wrote to me, enclosing some ruminations on Minnesota winters past, from his new perch as a snowbird in Arizona, of all places. "I'm here, and liking it!" he wrote. Weeks later, on his way back to his hometown of Minneota, he collapsed in the Sioux Falls airport, and was gone shortly thereafter. I wish that I had been there to catch him as he fell.

Of course, a special "Thank you" is in order, to all of the talented writers who made Volume Three (and all the other volumes) of Otter Tail Review possible.

Tim Rundquist
July 23, 2009

---

1   Where, during Ted and Mary's wedding reception, there was a significant diaper failure, resulting in clothing changes for both myself and a child who shall remain nameless (no need for further embarrassment).

2   It's up to you, readers, to locate these hotspots for yourselves. I'd recommend spreading that vintage county map onto the floor and looking for the more indirect, creative ways to get from Fergus to Otter Tail. Who knows, you may even get lost!

—To Bill Holm (1943-2009): mentor and friend, and a Minnesota landmark in his own right.

PART ONE

Winter Facts

by Bill Holm

The first fact on January Third
is the fact of winter,
more than dead banks, lost wars,
violence erupting here and there.
The fundamental fact is snow.
Is the glacier coming or going?
One man who loves the weather channel
watches the whole electronic map
swallowed up by snow
bite by bite until it's white
with fallen snow on snow
as the old hymn says,
and this first fact of winter
plants its icy boots on us.
Not forever, but long enough
to make us think.

Ingoji Gaa Pi Bizaanendamaan (A Place Where I Found Peace)

by Alex DeCoteau[1]

Gaa agaashiinyiyaan, aapiji ingii segiz. Mii go dibishkoo go aki gaa naniizaanak. Mii go gwiinawi inendamaan. Mii go gaye enendamaan ge ani izhiwebak ge ako bimaadiziyaan. Mii sa go iw, gaa onji minwendanziwaambaan.

When I was small, I was very scared. It was like the world was dangerous. I didn't know what to think. And I thought that was the way it was going to be for the rest of my life. So because of that, I was unhappy.

Mii dash ingoding gaa izhiwizhiyangid niimi'iding noosinaan. Ni minjimendaan gaa izhi ayaamagak. Mii endazhi niimi'iweng mewinzha. Mii go ginwenzh gaa ako niimi'idiwaad imaa.

Then one time our dad took us to the Pow-Wow. I remember the way it was. It was where they danced a long time ago. It's been a long time since they danced there.

Niminjimendam waabamagwaa ininiwag onaakosidoowaad mitigoonsan ogijayi'ii maa agwanogaaning. Booch igo gaa izhichigewaad i'iw eyindaso waa niimi'idiwaajin.

I remember seeing some men setting sticks on top of the arbor. They had to do that every time there was a dance.

Ingii niisakiipizomin imaa basanikaang ji dagoshinaang imaa. Besho gaa zhi noogibizoyaang. Ozhiitaawaad igo wii niimi'idiwaad. Noosinaan ezhi gaganoonaad anooji awiiyan.

We drove down into the ditch to get there. We parked up close. They were getting reading to dance. Our dad was talking to some of the guys.

Aapiji gagaanwaawan mashkosiwan ezhi gabaa'igooyaang odaabaaning. Mii go gaa pabaa wiiji'idiyaang imaa mashkosing. Mii go ezhi gaazoyaang, mikaadiyaang, bimibatooyaang, aazhikweyaang igaye. Aapiji dibenindizoyaang indagonaan. Mii go gaa moozhitooyaan iw noodin, ezhi mashkawaag igaye.

The grass was very tall as we were let off from the car. We played around with each other in the grass. We hid, we found each other, we ran, and we hollered. It was like we were completely free. I felt the wind and it was strong.

Gomaapi go, mii go waasa gaa izhi onjibatooyaan iw niimi'idiwigamigong. Mii go gaa izhi debitawag aw dewe'igan. Mii go ezhi ombishkaamagak inzhagayi'ii miziwe. Gichi gegoo inakamigad wenendamaan. Mii go ezhi maajaamagak babikwaazheyaan, ezhi noondawagwaa negamojig. Indigo go kina gegoo mino ayaamagad. Mii ezhi boomeyaan.

After a while, I had run a long way from the dance arena. I could hear the drum. My skin rose all over. I realized that something special was happening. And then my goose bumps went away as I heard the singer. It was like everything was all right. I felt safe.

Niizh akiwan dibishkoo naawa'ayi'ii gaa izhi ayaayaambaan. Aapiji go gaa izhi bi bizaanendamaan. Gagiige waa izhi ayayaayaan imaa.

It was like I was between two worlds. I had become very much at peace. I wanted to stay there forever.

Mii ako gaa pi bimaadiziyaan, mii go pane go gaa izhi nandawaabandamaan eteg bizaanendamowin.

For the rest of my life, I was always looking for the place where there was peace.

> *Mii go iw iidog.*
> That must be all.

---

1   The italicized text is the Anishinaabe language of northern Minnesota's indigenous people..

Where I Live

by Lois Schaedler

Where I live the dirt is potting soil. Not like potting soil, but potting soil. One guy is selling his farm – one cubic yard at a time. I grow perennials shoulder to shoulder to discourage weeds, and have innumerable gardens which have cut my mowing time down by an hour. Most of my plants are not natives, although I do have a volunteer Jack in the Pulpit or two.

My 120-plus year old farmstead boasts three giant oaks in the yard and two remaining eighty-foot cottonwoods in my few acres of forest. Seven acres are under the plow, which I rent out to a local farmer. Unfortunately modern farming practices have lost over ten inches of top soil from these acres. It's a real crime.

Four miles west of my place is the furthest eastern shore of glacial Lake Agassiz. It was an actual lakeshore when the giant mammoths roamed. Today it's just a small hillock running north and south. Seven miles east and a bit north of that lies the town of Fertile, Minnesota, which sits amongst sand hills. Stunted oaks, many over a hundred years old, grow to heights of only twelve feet or so in the preserve just south of town.

Approximately twenty miles north of my place lie tall grass prairies; to the south bog lands and buck brush divide myself from Mahnomen, a town on the White Earth Indian Reservation, where I am the local librarian for the Lake Agassiz Regional Library system, which covers an area the size of New Jersey, serving about 130,000 residents. Fosston, twenty-some-odd miles to the northeast boasts of being "where the prairie meets the pine."

Wrong on both counts. That divide actually occurs between Lengby and Bagley further east— but who's to argue with advertising?

Where I live the water is clean. I have a river running beneath my farm and my well is only seventy-five feet deep. Shallow by neighboring standards. The air is clean, most coming from Canada a mere hundred and ten miles to the north. Years ago the National Lampoon called Canada the "retarded giant at our doorstep." The Canadian government promptly banned the magazine.

My farm is populated by Sparky the dog, Momma Kitty the cat, a big black bear, an under-the-shed resident woodchuck, squirrels, rabbits, birds, butterflies, snakes (a few of which I consider pets), and deer. There are owls and bald eagles as well. We all live happily together.

I love to travel, but the greatest joy is always returning to my home of the past twenty-five years with the old two-story house and its poured-glass windows, including the one in the living room with the sand-blasted picture of two lovers flirting over a bucket of water at the watering trough with a cow looking on. This is where I live, and it is well-blessed.

A mile and a half south of my house runs the Sand Hill River. Years ago we'd catch big Northern pike there. They disappeared for a time, but rumor has it they're back. I'll be trying my luck in the near future.

Many lakes adorn the area, and several of my friends have cabins on some, and are gracious enough to give me free access any time I please.

Mahnomen, twenty-four miles south, houses a casino. I figure I'm just outside the "circle of crime," for I leave home traveling and never lock the door. My neighbor comes over daily to feed the pets, and my older Caddie (I have two late '80s models) sits in the drive with the keys in it. My long driveway keeps the dust from the gravel road from making its way to my house, the lawn-surrounding trees block the winter winds, and the circle drive (with no garage) affords me parking within two feet of the sidewalk and steps up to the porch. Sparky is trained to open the porch door on my command, so I can catch it with my elbow and make my way in laden with sundries. Sound idyllic? It is.

The giant willow, the only tree in the front yard when I bought the place, died and I left the big old trunk where it fell. Underneath live my snakes, and all around I've just planted a small grove of various lilac species. A hedge of lilacs I planted the year I bought the place now towers to twenty feet, and another type of lilac runs at a ninety-degree angle – just as tall – blooming at a later time. A "new" willow was planted out front about eight years ago and now is as tall as the house. A few barn-red outbuildings are scattered throughout the backyard.

Farms dot the landscape amongst the deciduous forests. The land was once completely covered by these forests, only to succumb to their destruction when, in the late 1800s, the Norwegians immigrated here. Garrison Keillor noted, "They moved to Minnesota because it reminded them of home. But the winters were much worse." For heat I have an oil-burning furnace, purchased used from the Grand Forks Air Force base for $157, and an old pot-bellied wood-burning stove in the living room. The kitchen holds my 1930s era cook stove. I have running water and a tub on feet.

If you're ever in the area, do stop by, you're all welcome. Just let me know when you're coming so I can introduce you to Sparky. She's real big and part wolf, friendly if you know her.

Getting to Me

by Linda M. Johnson

To get to my house,
take the Little Store exit.
Go north about three blocks.
School will be on your right,
kitty-corner from that the gas station
we call our small town's mini-mall.
Head west on '61, cross the Midway River.
Just past the feed store take a right.
From the highway watch for the tall,
skinny pine about a mile down.
We're the white house on the hill
across from the tractor place.

Getting to me is even easier,
just watch for signs.
Look into my eyes, you'll see longing.
Gaze awhile, you might also see hope.
Speak heartfelt words; at the smile continue.
When you see open arms meet me.
Tell me you love me.
Look no further.
My heart beating before you
will be yours then and there.

The House Where I Was Twelve

by Thomas R. Smith

That year, books and records seemed to over-
grow the back bedroom I shared with Terry.
Sometimes I dream of a drawer crammed with small

things I collected, but waking can't remember
what they were. Storms and flowers arrived
together when winter's hold loosened. The evening

the tornado ripped up Colfax, Dad herded us
to the basement where we leaned against dank walls.
He slipped on wet stairs, hit his head, got up.

We were alley pirates, plotted mischief
in an abandoned schoolbus up on blocks;
one day a pale drunk sprawled on the seats scared us.

Behind the locker plant, gut barrels stank
in the sun. At the garage, we watched the welder
in his smoked mask work blackened magic.

I developed a crush on the new girl next door,
with her glossy brown ponytail and
flashing smile. She was in my grade but

going steady with a letter-jacketed
upperclassman. I was ready for love,
but apparently love wasn't yet ready for me.

Though green winds tore the sky, an apple tree
outside our back bedroom window flourished
its bright promise. Warm spring rain raging

apple blossoms to earth also hastened the fruit.
Suddenly it became a matter of great
urgency to acquire a typewriter and a guitar.

Natural Features of Home

by Stash Hempeck

I have lived in my present house, on my current piece of property, my 150 x 150 foot lot, for twenty years now, the longest period of time I have ever occupied one single spot on earth. This ground is nestled in a small town—a village really—not quite one mile east of the Red River of the North, on the Minnesota side. It rests on the bottom of old, glacial Lake Agassiz, which at various times of its existence, managed to cover most of Manitoba, parts of eastern Saskatchewan and western Ontario, the eastern third of North Dakota, and most of northwestern Minnesota. In other parts of this geography, the glaciers scoured the earth, digging out what would become deep lakes and spitting out deposits of glacial moraine now called gravel pits; here, for various geological reasons, the lake bottom filled with sediment, silt that in time, after the waters receded, would help create a tall-grass prairie, home to some of the most fertile farmland in the world. Or so America would proudly—almost defiantly—proclaim to the world, when, after the Civil War, the first settlers and their children began to turn under the tall-grass sod, converting hundreds of years of natural decay into a few short decades of banner—no bumper—crops of wheat and barley.

Like its Minnesota cousin, the short-grass prairie where I grew up—prairie that lies to the south and east of The Valley, as everyone who lives here calls it, trees are rare commodities. Stories abound about the earliest settlers, mostly male, telling the later arrivals, again, mostly male, who might be looking for a wife, that there was a woman behind every tree. The kicker to the story, of course, was that the man first needed to find a tree. And unless the settler had managed to arrive early and homestead next to a river, he was, of course, quite out of luck in that regard. Perhaps that is why I think, in my more quirky or perhaps even more morbid moments of imagination, men first started planting trees in the valley.

My land in this village, when I came into ownership of it, happened to be graced with a rather large number of trees: five crown-spreading elms on the south side cast a long rectangle of shade all summer; eight rougher looking ash on the west did the same, while also providing shade for the house from the heat of the late afternoon sun; up against the alley on the north, four more ash and two box elder helped break the winter winds. On one side of the driveway that entered between the elms from the south grew a magnificent oak, the kind early settlers lusted after to cut numerous long, straight boards, while across from it on the other side towered a twenty-five foot White Pine, with its perfect Christmas tree shape, the type those settlers' descendents lusted after every December. Only on the east was the lot clear of any growth, clear to show the horizon turn from red to orange to gold, as the orb of the sun rose higher and higher into the ever-changing blue hues of the morning sky.

Still, the number of trees was not enough for me. Perhaps it was the fact that after years on non-ownership of any land, of not being able to design a yard I felt comfortable in, of hating the task of mowing all that damn grass from all those damn lawns—to what end I could never figure out—that the dam holding back the waters of my creative energies finally broke and began to flood the property. Perhaps it was guilt from all the years I cut down live trees, which I then trimmed and blocked and split and stacked, to then burn during the late-fall, winter, and early-spring months to keep myself warm; to cook my meals, especially the fresh cornmeal muffins or multi-grain flapjacks of breakfast; to make my ever-present tea kettle ready to sing at a moment's notice. Or perhaps, it was the simple wisdom I remembered from an episode of the TV show Bonanza, where Ben Cartwright's middle son Hoss tells a visitor, that his "Paw don't let nobody cut down a tree without first planting one to replace it."

In any case, I, too, began to plant. For the first time, I made use of the free trees that went with my annual Arbor Day membership. Year One I put in a dozen lilacs on the east half of the south side, the first step to creating a natural hedge. Year Two I planted a dozen white pine between the ash of the west side, preparing for the day when those ash trees would no longer be there. Year Three, on the north side, by the alley, I planted a dozen cedar seedlings, foot-high experiments I rescued from the dumpster behind one of the greenhouses at North Dakota State University. Year Four, I transplanted six ash and four box elder that had sprouted along the edge of the garden, and which I hadn't had the heart to uproot, to what I felt were appropriate spots elsewhere in the yard. Year Five, more lilacs, this time on the west side, just in front of the old ash and young white pine, to start another hedge there. And so it went.

There were, of course, setbacks. No matter how much care and attention I lathered on them, some young trees simply died. Dutch Elm Disease ravished the beauties on the south side some years ago, leaving, inexplicably, only the center elm, though it, too, now shows the inevitable signs of its approaching death: discoloration in the bark of the trunk, a rather sick-looking gray compared to the light brown it should be; the dead small branches higher up, denuded of all foliage, that break off in the slightest wind; the clumps of discolored leaves an odd mix of mostly yellow with some off-green, both of which are covered in brown spots of varying size and shade, none of which would look out of place in September or October, but which are a sure sign of distress in mid-summer.

The high winds—"straight-line" they have come to be called—of three summer storms brought down four of the ash on the west, leaving a gaping hole, an open wound that now heats the house in summer, causing the central air system to work overtime in June, July and August.

And then there are those, in retrospect, humorous-but-still-serious occasions, as when my eldest son, age eight at the time, eager to prove his responsibility, asked to mow the lawn. And ten minutes into his task, looking, no doubt, for approval, asked how he was doing, while simultaneously running over and shredding, in quick succession, first a lilac, then a white pine, then another lilac.

But I kept at it, this process of bringing these foreign lives onto the prairie. For years I longed for an orchard. Ten years ago some good friends grafted fresh branch ends from their most productive plum tree onto three plum suckers that had sprouted in their lawn and gifted their efforts to me. One of these died, but the other two grew and produced bright, reddish-purple plums with bitter skins but golden, juicy insides. At least until one of the storms that felled some of the ash threw my sons' trampoline through one tree, and severely damaged numerous branches on the other. In spite of careful pruning of both, the former now dies one or two limbs a year, while the latter has yet to recover its full vigor. In fact, last year it showed ample signs of a disease that I think is black rot, which, if so, will necessitate my cutting it down. This spring I started the grafting process all over again on my own suckers.

Six years ago I planted five apple trees, five different varieties. They, too, did beautifully, until The Winter of the Rabbits. Prior to that year, the town I live in was cottontail free, but that January they appeared out of nowhere, like the biblical plagues of old. I was luckier than most in the town; while all my apple trees were attacked, only four suffered minor damage before I noticed—the exception being the Haralson, where one or more rabbits girdled the bark almost the entire way around, a strip five inches high. Only a narrow three-quarter-inch band kept the life-giving connection between root and branch going long enough for the tree to heal itself.

Five falls back, the oak dropped a copious crop of acorns, more than any year before or since. That following spring I dug up a dozen sprouts, before their tap roots went down too deep to make transplanting a viable option. Most went to the west side. Two died of unknown causes, three were destroyed by rabbits; but the survivors grew straight and true, and even now are working to help fill in that open wound left by the passing storms of the past.

And the last two years I have fought a relentless battle with the long-eared enemy among the hazelnut bushes, another project courtesy of the Arbor Day Foundation. Each spring I planted four bushes, only to see, no matter what I did, that only a sole survivor came up the following spring. This year I was told the replacements will be shipped in the fall; perhaps that change of pace will allow for less of a death rate.

After all these endeavors over the past twenty years, I know that I do not plant these foreign lives in this prairie soil because I am looking for a wife; I already have one of those. Nor do I plant these trees in an attempt to tame this prairie, which was conquered by humans many years ago—in a sense, even before the white settlers came—though I often believe the land would be better off with the sound and movement of tall grass and the smell of generations of sod, rather than being caught in the throes of the agri-chemical menagerie of corn, soybeans, sugar beets, and wheat. And I do not plant these trees because I wish to stake claim of ownership. In the natural scheme of things, twenty years is nothing.

Therefore, I do not question my actions anymore; nor do I attempt to understand them. I simply accept, that, for whatever reason or reasons, I am addicted to trees. No doubt addiction is not the proper word, conjuring up, as it most often does, the harsh and negative images of alcoholics in doorways, or tourniquets and needles in back alleys. Besides, when I am planting and tending and burying this flora, I am quite certain that I do not feel, like I imagine a methamphetamine or crack-cocaine addict feels. Still, if I think of my actions these past years as habit, compulsion, obsession, need, craving, infatuation, perhaps even dependence, it seems to me I cannot help but come back to addiction.

Last week, when out walking around in the yard, I attempted to count—

including the ones that died—the number of trees and bushes I have placed into this prairie earth. I quit after I reach one hundred.

Still, as I gave one last glance around, there is some open space yet on the south, and on the west, and on the north. And someone recently gave me some black walnuts that were stored inside all last winter. They will need seasoning first, of course, put through the cold of this winter to stratify them.

And then, next spring . . .

What You Noticed the Last Time You Passed Through

by Mark Vinz

Both bars are still open, dueling their
Bud Light neon; both gas stations, too,
plus the one out by the highway
with its new mini-mart. The fourth is now
a beauty shop and tanning salon.

No doctor's office any more, but
the chiropractor is still next door
to the weekly newspaper. There's a
big metal building called an Event Center
where the bowling alley used to be,
the grocery store rents videos and DVDs,
the old brick bank is home to antiques and
collectibles. Some of the streets have been
given names: Ash and Elm and Main.

The house is gone, of course, a vacant lot
with weeds, but still a clump or two of rhubarb
and one corner of the lilac hedge. A block away
two dozen trains still rumble by each day,

though none will ever stop. As for the schools,
they're empty now, consolidated, moved to
other towns. Only the café and the funeral home
have added on. The last class numbers peeling
on the water tower are more than ten years old.

Pilgrimage

by Rasma Haidri

His name was Lars Andersen, his father Anders Larsen, whose father
again was named Lars Andersen, and so on went the record of my great-
grandfather's ancestry in the hand written church directories I found in
the Norwegian National Archives in Oslo in 1980 when I was a new bride,
a reverse-immigrant gone back to the land from whence my grandparents
came, gone back to learn to use my hands to knit sweaters and weave
placemats and bake whole grain bread the way every modern Norwegian
woman must and can

but not my grandmother Anna, daughter of Lars, not my own mother,
daughter of Anna, no, the Norwegian immigrant daughters raised on
Wisconsin tobacco farms bought their sweaters in Madison on the Square
and ate Wonder Bread and puffed rice and spoke of Norway like a fairytale
land that ceased to exist when the last of them came, Lars Andersen the
last in a long line of Norwegian seacoast men with no family name other
than "son of the father named so and so" - Lars and Anders sufficing for
generations until my grandfather emigrated to Amerika with two daughters
and no son

having fled Kristiansund for killing a man, something about throwing
him overboard into the sea, but no one really knows for sure, no one ever
knows these immigrant stories do they, not the whole of them, only bits
passed on and altered in the retelling, Anna was five when they came,

she remembered the sea of wild waves, then later being confirmed in the Norwegian Synod Lutheran church on the same Dakota prairie where her sister, dead of appendicitis at age twelve, was buried

I have a photograph of Lars Andersen hovering over the coffin like a giant hewn out of rough wood, another shows the horse-drawn hearse and a line of mourners plodding behind in clod boots, I have the brass-hinged Norwegian bible in gothic script where Lars Andersen's baptism is recorded on gossamer, I have the milk table from the barn that didn't burn when the rest of the farm did, and on the edge of the table I have the treasure that appeared when I removed the thick black paint: my grandmother's name carved with straight blade gashes like a child's printed script - A-N-N-A

but will you understand me when I say that what I really want is the green and white road sign that marks the half-mile long lane of asphalt running between fields just off Wisconsin County C and Highway 16, the signpost that says Andersen Road and points to the farm that burned down, where everything they had brought from Norway was lost in a fire that raged in five buildings until the men in the fields heard the horses scream

my grandmother used to say Nei det e ikkje greit å være i Amerika! whenever someone dropped a cup or stubbed a toe, No, it's not all that great being here in America! she would chuckle, drumming her fingers on the table, nodding her head in confirmation of the old immigrant truth, Nei det e ikkje greit å være i Amerika was the only Norwegian any of us heard

until I reverse-emigrated at twenty-one and set about learning my grandparents' tongue through books checked out from the Oslo city library, fairy tales and grade school primers, but when a letter came from Wisconsin saying I am sorry to tell you grandmother is dead, I wept because I hadn't learned enough Norwegian yet, I had wanted to show her I could speak her language, take her on a pilgrimage back to our heritage, let her chuckle that things were not so great in America, let her see that Norway was not just a tale her father told his one remaining child

but when I returned to Wisconsin she was already buried in the cemetery at Bonnet Prairie where her father Lars Andersen was also buried, as was his wife who came with him from Norway, as later would be their grandchildren, my mother and all her brothers, all the sons and daughters of Norway buried under red granite tombstones just a mile as the crow flies from Andersen Road it is the one place I would say I want to visit before I die, go back to Andersen Road and look at that sign, but no let me be honest, I would do vandalism to it, take a sledgehammer and knock it out of the ground, or if that didn't work I'd shinny up the gray pole and unscrew the bolts, dissever the joints with a torch, I would take my great-grandfather's name from its neglected post and bring it home to my yard on the Norwegian coast, erect it facing the sea and claim it as my own: Great-granddaughter of Lars Son-of-Anders, this is her road

The Sauna At Twelve-Foot

by Marlene Mattila Stoehr

On the banks of the Red Eye River, by the bridge
near the deep spot known simply as Twelve-Foot,
stood my grandparents' sauna.
Gone now, not even the grass-lined path remains.
Gone, parades of people each Saturday night,
partakers in the ritual that is the Finnish sauna.
We knew who would be there, and the order in which they would bathe;
family and friends, carrying stiff, line-dried towel bundles,
fresh clothing wrapped within.
Gone, pine benches and woven rag rugs in the dressing room,
and pine walls where youth scrawled names and initials
with the cork from Grandma's bottle of Mrs. Stewart's Liquid Bluing.

A kerosene lamp on a shelf beside a small, square window
cast a soft light into the steam room.
Naked bathers on slatted, tiered benches
threw dippers of water at hot rocks cradled on the stove,
creating clouds of cleansing steam - the essence of the sauna.
Whisks, fashioned in early summer from leafy birch branches
and carefully bound together with a single supple branch,
soaked in a bucket of water. Steamed on hot rocks,
they released their fresh, summery fragrance all year long as
bathers switched their bodies to make hot skin even hotter,

until at last they opened a vent high on the back wall
and let in cool, fresh air and a chorus of familiar river sounds.
Bathers lathered with the bar of red Lifebuoy soap,
rinsed with buckets of water and, after drying and dressing,
filled the sauna stove with wood and the galvanized water tubs
with water from the Red Eye.

Returning to the house, people complimented Grandma on the sauna,
as one would compliment a good cook on her cooking.
Adults sat around the oilcloth-covered kitchen table
drinking hot coffee from large white cups, or, following local custom,
from saucers balanced on two knuckles and a thumb,
sipping through sugar lumps from the glass bowl on the table.
A kerosene lamp cast a yellow circle before them as they spoke,
sometimes in Finnish, sometimes in English,
for some knew only one language
and some topics were covered only in Finnish
in deference to the children playing in the darkened living room.
Conversations in Finnish drew Grandpa from his chair by the window
where he watched headlights and taillights of arriving or departing cars.
Grandma circled between the table, the coffeepot on the woodstove,
and the Hoosier cupboard with the crock of sugar cookies.

Late in the rotation, our family bathed. Then my father, the oldest son,
was entrusted to shave his father and trim his mustache
with exacting strokes of the ivory-colored straightedge razor.
Sleepy children, yet we watched, drawn by the aroma of the shaving soap
and the soft clink of the shaving brush against the chipped china cup.
When at last alone, my grandparents took their Saturday sauna.
As the fire died down for another week, they would rest on the pine
benches,
then blow out the lamp and walk together along the familiar path to the
silent house.

Today the Red Eye River flows on, though its flow is greatly diminished.
The bridge with its iron railing is replaced by a concrete culvert.
The river sounds are muted, and Twelve-Foot a location few remember.
That sauna, that path, those people are gone. But in other homes and other
places,
the ancient Finnish tradition yet survives.

Cat, Fish in the Bedroom

by Kathy Coudle King

TIME:

April, 1997

PLACE:

A modest home in Grand Forks, North Dakota

Action takes place in the living room. There is a recliner, a lamp on a table, and the rest of the room is stacked with cardboard boxes, some which block the sight of a TV.

CHARACTERS:

> RON - a middle-aged political science professor, cynical and laid back.

> LINDA - his middle-aged wife, a planner who likes to have her "ducks in a row."

They've been married for a good 20-something years, long enough to have grown children living on their own.

Ron is in his Lazy Boy, remote control by his side, TV softly playing a news show. He is reading the newspaper. The area around him is stacked with packing boxes.

Linda enters from s.l., sweaty and disheveled. She is carrying a large box. She stares at Ron then drops the box with a loud thud. Ron looks up at her over his newspaper. She "huffs," turns on her heel, and walks out s.l.. Ron resumes reading. Linda is heard off stage stomping around. She returns momentarily with another large box. She stares at Ron, but he does not look up. She drops the box with a thud. Ron does not register the noise.

LINDA: Here's the thing: the river is rising and *you* don't know how to swim.

RON: And?

LINDA: *I* know how to swim.

RON: Yes?

LINDA: If there's a flood, I have *survival skills*, but you –

RON: I have survival skills. I *shopped.*

LINDA: (reaches into a box and pulls out a can of beans)
           Beans? You think beans are going to save your stinking ass?

RON: Pork *and* beans.

LINDA tosses the beans at him. He catches it.

RON: Hey! You almost put my eye out with those beans.

LINDA: The great survivalist is going to simply camp out while the river floods his town!

RON: How many times do I have to tell you: It's not going to flood.

LINDA: Oh, and you know this because . . . you teach political science?

RON: Look, the river *might* flood, but we're not going to get any water in the house. We never get any water. Did we in '79? In '85? I'm telling you, we're not going to get any water. (Resumes reading his paper.)

LINDA: Oh, yeah? Then why are we forced to carry flood insurance?

RON: Some Corp of Engineers dope drew a map based on some cockamamie calculations and the bank laps them up. It's all part of an insurance scam, anyway.

LINDA: A scam? Flood insurance is a scam.

RON: You got it, toots.

LINDA: The whole town is evacuating, the Hansons evacuated yesterday, the Dillards the day before, but you think it's all a scam?

RON: The Hansons are a couple of Henny Pennies – "The sky is falling, the sky is falling," and Jake Dillard confided he's hoping to get a little fishing in up at his cabin. They're using the flood as an excuse to take off from work, dear. Wake up and smell the coffee. Speaking of, I wouldn't mind a cup right about now. You?

LINDA: The whole damn town has been sand bagging for two-weeks. Has that been a scam, too?

RON: Somebody's making money on that sand. And the bags. Betcha life on it.

LINDA: You're impossible!

RON: And you're naive. What you need to do is watch more TV. Say, would you step aside, Dr. Phil's about to come on.

LINDA does so, shaking her head, and Ron points the remote control at the TV.

V.O.:   Today on *Dr. Phil*: When you and your partner have different sexual needs.

RON snorts. Linda begins to exit. A frantic BEEP-BEEP-BEEP.

ANNOUNCER: This is the 9-1-1 operator. The Riverside dyke has been breached. I repeat, the Riverside dyke has been breached.
(Her voice cracks)
E-evacuate immediately. All residents and volunteers are ordered by the National Guard to evacuate immediately. (Pause) God bless.

LINDA begins grabbing first one box, then another.
RON jumps up.

LINDA: Grab something, the wedding albums, no, the Christmas decorations, wait, the kids' baby books! Oh, grab anything!

RON: Did you hear that?

LINDA: Yes, evacuate, e-vacuate – now!

RON: The 9-1-1 operator said, "God bless." She's not allowed to say that!

LINDA: Oh, my books! My books are still in the basement!

RON: The frigging 9-1-1 operator said, "God bless." Damn, I think she was crying.

LINDA: We'll take the van. No, the car is newer. But the van will
              fit more! Grab something!

              She rushes out s.l. with a box. Ron looks around and
              grabs a box, opens the lid. Holds up a can. It's the beans.
              He stuffs it back in box and runs into Linda coming in; he
              exits. Linda scurries around, peeking into boxes, decides
              on one as Ron returns.

RON: Only the essentials.

              She exits. He looks around in his chair, retrieves remote
              control and tosses it in a box, exits with it.

              LINDA returns, out of breath, picks up box, then puts it
              down. She gets down on her hands and knees, looking low,
              making "spp" sounds.

LINDA: Gloria? Here, baby, here, Gloria!

              RON enters from s.l., going straight for another box, and
              stumbles over Linda.

RON: What the – are you taking a nap? Grab a box. The cars will
              be backed up to the Interstate. Friggin' 9-1-1 operator is
              going to cause a stampede.

LINDA: I am not leaving without Gloria! Here, kitty, mama's not
              mad at you, here, Gloria!

RON: Don't worry about the cat. She's got 9 lives.

              Ron grabs a box and goes out with it. Gloria stays in
              position, making kissy sounds. Ron returns.

RON (cont.):   Geez, Linda, forget about the damn cat! We've
                   gotta get going – now.

LINDA: I am not leaving Gloria. She hates water.

RON: Yeah, me, too.

LINDA: She can't swim.

RON: Me either. Now, come on.

LINDA: No.
           (she begins crawling between the boxes, making kissy
           sounds)

RON: Linda, I swear, if you don't –

LINDA: Are you going to leave me here?
           (Pause)

RON: What? You can swim.

LINDA: Bastard!
           (She continues to crawl)

RON: It was a joke. To break the tension?
           (sighs, then gets down on his knees)

LINDA: You and the jokes. Always with the jokes. You know? You
           don't respond properly to situations. The mayor, the Corp
           of Engineers, the flippin' National Guard says to evacuate,
           but what do you say? You say, "It's a scam" and turn on
           Dr. Phil.

RON: Look, the only reason I'm evacuating is to humor you.
           Worse case scenario, we lose our power for a couple days,
           a week tops. I've stocked up on batteries. *I've* got canned
           goods.

LINDA: Yeah, you're a regular boy scout, you are. Spp, spp!

RON: What, you think I couldn't survive for a few days? Think
           I couldn't defend my house?

LINDA: Don't yell; that's why she's hiding. She hates raised
           voices.

RON: Yeah, well, I hate –

LINDA: Shh! Be sweet. Gloria responds to sweet.

RON: Sweet? The river is flooding, and we –

LINDA: Sweet.

RON (in a falsetto): Oh, Gloria! Where are you? Here pussy, pussy!

> LINDA and RON continue to crawl between the boxes. An air-raid siren goes off somewhere off stage. Both sit up and listen.

RON: Oh, damn, Linda we –

LINDA   (frantically)
           Gloria, spp, spp, spp!
           (She gestures for Ron to join her)

RON (frantically):   Here, kitty, kitty, we're going to drown if you don't come out right now!

LINDA (stands up: She's not here.

RON: No, she's probably high and dry in a tree. That's where we're going to be if we don't get moving.

> LINDA walks to s.r..

LINDA: She's probably under our bed.
           (Exits)

RON: No!

LINDA (O.S.):   Gloria!

> RON looks around at the boxes then bends over to grab one and cries out in pain, grabbing the base of his back. He does not straighten up.

RON: Lin-da! Linda!

He slowly moves to his chair, and with great effort he sits.

LINDA (O.S.):   Gloria! Why, you naughty kitty! Come to mama, come here sweet— Ow! You little bitch, I should leave you here to drown. No, wait! No, mama was – come back here, come on, damn it! Ron? Ron can you get me the pet carrier and – and a broom?

Ron puts his head back on the chair and closes his eyes. Over head is the sound of a helicopter.

RON (whispers):   Save me.

LINDA enters. Stares at him a beat, picks up an item and throws it at him. She misses.

RON (cont.):   I can't move.

LINDA: What? I can't believe you're going to pout because I won't leave the cat. Gloria means –

RON: My back. I threw out my back, for crying out loud!

LINDA: Now? Right now?

RON: Sorry to inconvenience you.

LINDA: You always have to be the center of attention, don't you? Natural disaster — step aside, Ronald Enger needs you to pay attention to him. Why, even when I was giving birth you couldn't stand not being in the spotlight. So what do you do? You throw out your back. I'm having your ten pound son, and you throw out your back. The nurses forgot about me; I might as well have had him alone in a cornfield as much help as I got, everyone fawning over you. Every —

RON: Linda, this has nothing –

LINDA: So sorry I haven't given you enough attention the last few

days, Ronnie. You see, me and the rest of our neighbors, we've been preparing for a flood. And today they've all evacuated, but me and you, we're still here. Forgive me if I don't want to leave without the only living thing in this house who gives a crap about me, that notices I'm still breathing. You just sit on your butt and think about insurance scams and conspiracy theories. Me? I'm getting Gloria and I'm going.
(She storms off s.l..)

RON: Linda! Linda! I'm not faking, I'm –

She returns with a pet carrier and a broom, shakes her head at him.

LINDA: Pathetic.

She storms past him and exits towards the bedroom.

RON: Linda! I'm serious, my back is locked. You know how it gets. I can't move. I can't walk, I –

There's a loud YEOW off stage.

RON (CONT.):   Linda?

Linda returns carrying pet carrier, looks at Ron and shakes her head.

LINDA: Pathetic.

RON: I am not kidding – I can't –

Linda walks out carrying the pet carrier, grabbing the lamp with the other arm.

RON (CONT.):   Linda! Please!

Off stage a car door is opened then slammed. An engine is started. A door opens and slams again.

RON: Linda, don't leave me!

            Linda returns.

LINDA: (shaking)
            I can see it, the water, it's down on Seventh Avenue! I'm
            taking the van. Here are the car keys!
            (She tosses them to him)

            She runs off s.r., returning momentarily with a gold fish
            bowl filled with water and a fish.

LINDA: Almost forgot Goldie! Not that she'd mind a flood.
            (Laughs hysterically)

RON: Please, honey, listen to me. I –

LINDA: Ron, you really need help with this attention thing. We'll
            talk later. Meet me at my mother's! No more screwing
            around, now. Shake a leg!
            (She grabs a box in spare hand and exits)

RON: My back, Linda, it's locked and I –

            A door slams, tires squeal.

RON: Linda!

            Then it's just the sirens. He shoves back, softly at first, then
            getting up a good rock, eventually he catapults himself out
            of his chair, onto his hands and knees and crawls to s.r.
            during the following.

RON: Gotta get – to higher ground. Gotta get – the bedroom,
            gotta get to – it won't reach. No, just a little basement
            damage, not first floor, certainly not — be okay. Higher
            ground. Higher ground.

                          LIGHTS

                          THE END

Going to Berea

by Karen Loeb

You are lost.

The man in the gas station
whittles a bird.
After a long time he says,
"If you don't know where
you're going
you should stay home."

You return to your car
a new woman
determined to find Berea
despite being geographically
challenged.

After a while—it could be
hours—you realize the
path you have chosen
will get to Berea by way
of China or Pakistan.

You inform your three
passengers.

They coo in your ear
about the scenic route
being so much nicer.
You suspected from the start
that they were polite.
You are undaunted
by their clamoring to see
the Golden Gate Bridge
and pandas in their native
habitat.

You turn the car around
and head back
looking for Berea or at least
a sign pointing there.

A man along the road
training thoroughbreds
says the sign to Berea
blew away in a tornado
and no one put it up again.

You think he nods
in the direction you're headed
but you might be standing
at an odd angle
or he might be upside down
and you haven't noticed.

To Love This Town

by Laura L. Hansen

You ask me what it is like to love this town
as one who grew up here, not as you - a newcomer - love it,
but as one who has known it forever, one whose memories of it include
the soft days of youth. So I close my eyes and remember.

I remember each building and old friend,
each trip to the city beach, the old high school crew,
the nights cruising around for hours on a dollar's worth of gas,
the clang and rattle of foul balls hitting the chain link fence behind home
plate, the neighborhood bikes piled up like junkyard dogs in front of the
house.

I touch them each, moving each memory along the palm of my hand
like a daisy chain - he loves me, he loves me not - alternating
and reassuring, re-experiencing, and feeling for what's been lost.
Things have changed. We've progressed. Who, after all, could really miss
the three-story brick Junior High with floors so steeply pitched that our
pencils always rolled off our desks.

What I do miss is the uninterrupted view across the river, back when the
sun
set by weaving bold colors through the tops of trees instead of dropping
its spotlight eye abruptly down behind the new county garage. I miss

A&W Tater Tots and a frosty mug hung on trays from the side of the car
and wearing some boys jacket to stay warm as we sat on the side hill
at the football games, away from the bleachers and the bleacher's bright
lights.

I miss life without I-Pods and cell phones, when the people you were
talking to listened instead of glancing furtively, boldly, blatantly away to
check messages.
I miss quiet. As I age, everyone seems too loud, too forward, too....
much.
What was it you asked me? I've lost the drift. You didn't ask me what I miss,
but how I love it now - this town of ours - and how it was to love it then.

Simple. It was simple to love it then, for what else did I really know? Love,
separated from any other reality, was inevitable. As it is now.

Water Street Bridge and the Struggle to Save an Otter Tail County Landmark

by Matthew Hoekstra

Cursed be he that removeth his neighbor's landmark.
Deuteronomy 27:17

For a growing number of individuals, preservation of local sites induces a recollection of their past — to their childhood, a favorite spot, or a retreat. Historic sites anchor collective memories by providing tangible evidence of the past. People visit them, according to sociologist Diane Barthel, to "get in touch with history" in a very real, literal sense. Preservation offers an unfiltered approach to history.[1]

In Otter Tail County, Minnesota, in the late 1970s and early 1980s, preservation was at the fore of political and public debate. The issue was whether or not Maine Township should replace the historic Water Street Bridge. For many, this local landmark was worthy of preservation. What followed was an impressive grassroots effort by individuals of varied backgrounds — to save Water Street Bridge. Not only that, this episode reveals much about society and culture in rural west central Minnesota.

In 1978, the Otter Tail County Commissioners were making

arrangements to replace "deficient" bridges throughout the county. Due to a number of bridge collapses throughout the country, the state legislature enacted a bridge bonding program in 1976 whereby the state would pick up most of the tab for bridge replacement. Local governments, unsurprisingly, responded. As of February 1980, 4,000 bridges in Minnesota had been replaced. However, since the Otter Tail River is a navigable stream, the U.S. Army, Corps of Engineers would have the final say.[2]

As pressure mounted on the bridge, some local residents organized. At least thirty residents joined the newly incorporated Water Street Bridge Preservation Society, Inc. Members included local residents of all backgrounds, including farmers, back-to-the-landers, local professionals, lawyers, and outdoor enthusiasts. They were not, as depicted by Otter Tail County's 3rd District Commissioner, "a handful of out-of-state people, who have recently moved in, and Fergus Falls environmentalists…"[3]

As the Water Street Bridge Preservation Society formed, their concerns, as noted in a flyer advertising their mission, were centered on the cost of the potential project, water/traffic safety, environmental impact, ecological considerations, historic value of the bridge, and lastly, aesthetics. In addition, there were concerns about the economic impact that removal of the bridge would have on the local tourist industry. In fact, many persons from around the country who had fished from the bridge signed a petition to save it. Clearly, replacement of the bridge with culverts would have altered every one of the group's concerns.

Costs of the project initially had an estimate of $130-200,000 in 1980, with Maine Township responsible for at least $13,000. What proponents of replacement also failed to mention, according to editorials from the Fergus Falls Daily Journal and letters to the editor, was that the County Road and Bridge Fund was already $705,000 in the red in 1979-80. Many bridges were targeted due to the availability of state and federal money, so-called "free money." According to Otter Tail County Engineer Denis Berend, when the program started, "we really got aggressive. We'd be negligent in our duties if we didn't."[4] Therefore, the intention of the county government was to get what they could monetarily, regardless of the sentiments of the residents of Maine Township. In fact, before the township board had even voted, Alcoa Steel had already furnished Otter Tail County with engineering drawings at no cost, for steel culverts. In 1977, the bridge was rated at 8 out of a possible 9. But in 1978, once the "free money" was available, the rating curiously fell to 4, putting it on the deficient list. Although the township residents approved an initial vote to replace the bridge with a span bridge in March 1979 when they thought they had to replace it, the culverts were forced upon them by the county. Which is from where, likely, much of the opposition came.[5]

It was not just the cost of a bridge that concerned the Water Street Bridge Preservation Society and others— although it was steep, especially considering the state of the nation at that time. What also concerned them was the environmental impact on the water, plant, and animal life.

Members of the Water Street Bridge Preservation Society were not wrong in having environmental concerns regarding potential bridge replacement. In examining the Environmental Assessment (EA), it is clear that the author shared many of their concerns. The author noted that there would be, at best, "minor" adverse impact regarding air quality, wetlands, aquatic habitat diversity and interspersion, biological productivity, surface water quality, and soil degradation. While the EA reveals a laundry list of at least "minor" adverse environmental impact, Dr. Charles Carson (PhD in Geology), formerly Deputy Director of the Minnesota Pollution Control Agency, told a much different tale, noting that, "There is no way such a massive earth fill construction can be undertaken in a site like this without serious and probably irreversible damage to the surrounding lake bed, stream channel, and wild rice beds." Dr. Carson went on to add:

I cannot find a single redeeming feature in the proposed replacement of Water Street Bridge by earthen fill. It is a frivolous, expensive, destructive, and wasteful scheme, occupying the valuable time of engineers, earth movers, and the sellers of steel tubing, and the energy of those opposing such follies, when their energies might better be devoted to constructive ventures more in keeping with modern scientific ecology, engineering, and sound economic principles.[6]

In addition to the EA and the report of Dr. Carson, the testimony of individuals in similar situations, on the same river, was taken into account. They called attention to the effects of new culverts resulting in increased hazards to boaters, increased sediment in the river, disrupted fishing, and ruined wild rice crops. Others noted that they used the river less than they would have otherwise. One local resident stated, "They were trying to make it a scenic river a couple of years ago but now they've ruined a beautiful river with those culverts."[7]

Moreover, the local chapter of the Izaak Walton League, an environmental organization founded in 1922 to promote natural resource protection, "vigorously opposed the replacement of Water Street Bridge" with culverts. The Izaak Walton League, Otter Chapter, argued that the Federal Bridge Replacement Program should be subject to the same special use permits as shoreline.

When the Water Street Bridge Preservation Society argued that the historic value of the bridge would be destroyed, no one could argue that point. The removal of the bridge would have, in fact, removed a historic landmark that was nearly a century old. The bridge was named after Joe Water Street, an early resident of Otter Tail County, a fur trapper/trader and resort owner, and was built in 1910. The historic value went beyond simply its age. The historical record indicates that the design itself merited preservation due to the beauty of its construction, which allowed easy adjustment of the bridge and a redistribution of weight. According to Minnesota's State Historic Preservation Officer Russell Fridley, who toured the area in October of 1979, the bridge was a Pratt through-truss design and "among the oldest in the northwestern part of the state." Fridley went on to add that the bridge was "unique in at least a six county area."[8]

Moreover, the area surrounding the bridge was also historically significant for a number of reasons. First of all, it was on the earliest route from Fergus Falls to Perham. Further, the area was frequented by Native Americans who traveled the route and used the area as a camping ground. As a result of the historic properties of the bridge and area, the bridge was listed as eligible for nomination to the National Register of Historic Places in May 1980.[9]

It would be unfair to demonize all of those who favored replacement of the Water Street Bridge. After all, the Legislature's bridge bonding program authorized $127 million as a result of the Minnesota Department of Transportation identifying 5,000 out of 19,300 bridges as needing replacement. The problem was that the only bridge work being funded was replacement, not repairs. Therefore, the cash-strapped counties and townships jumped at the chance to receive state monies. Members of the Water Street Bridge Preservation Society recognized that the bridge needed work; however, they advocated for repair over replacement, which again, was not being funded through legislative sources.

So, what did the Water Street Bridge Preservation Society do? One way was to bring its message to the people. Not long after the Water Street Bridge Preservation Society was formed, members and Maine Twp. residents Joe and Elizabeth Merz, along with Dr. Tom Smith, addressed members of the Fergus Falls Kiwanis in August of 1979. Three months prior, Maine Township residents approved replacement with culverts – repairing the bridge was not put to the vote — and in July, the town board had authorized the county to move forward and replace the bridge. Now, local service clubs joined the Water Street Bridge Preservation Society members in taking their complaints to legislators about the state's bridge replacement program as a whole, not only of Otter Tail County's pursuit of Water Street Bridge. The legislature began a review of the bridge bonding program in December of 1979.

The group also invited the services of local and statewide historic experts in their preservation efforts. At the behest of local historians, the state historic society became involved. Preservation officials from the state historical society noted that the bridge warranted nomination to the National Register, which was important because nomination would assure careful consideration when work was done to alter it. At this point, county commissioner Andy Leitch personally authored a letter that was sent to Russell Fridley, State Historic Preservation Officer, suggesting that involvement with Water Street Bridge might "shut the doors of the Otter Tail County Museum, because of a lack of funds." He did not need to remind Fridley that the county museum depended upon the county for operating funds. Fridley responded with a letter of his own, which informed the commissioner that the historical society was "required by law to comment on effect of federally funded projects of historically significant properties." Leitch was not the only individual to make such a threat, which he called "more a little push." Like Leitch, township supervisor Don Roberts made a similar statement: "I think the position of the Minnesota Historical Society has jeopardized the Otter Tail County Historical Society."[10]

The Society also made effective use of the local media. There were many articles in the local newspaper, the Fergus Falls Daily Journal. Further, supporters of preservation submitted numerous erudite letters to the editor. The print media also came out in support of, if not preservation, at least a review of the current legislation, and a number of editorials criticized the current bridge replacement program. In fact, the editors pointed out that the county road and bridge program operated at a deficit.[11]

In May of 1980, the bridge topic continued to be divisive. At a public hearing of the Corps of Engineers on 15 May 1980, Corps officials heard testimony for and against preservation for more than two hours. Preservationists articulated a number of reasons that they hoped would influence the Corps' decision. First of all, they had acquired 160 signatures of eligible Maine Township voters who supported keeping the bridge. They also pointed out the historic merit of the bridge, as well as the environmental degradation that would be caused by the proposed 294-inch culverts and the granular fill. Further still, there was the cost, the loss of a recreation spot, the questioned durability of culverts, the legality of the county's approach, and the social value of the bridge. Opponents of preservation pointed to replacement as being in the public interest and "progressive." Others pointed out the deficiencies with the current bridge, which didn't allow for smooth transportation for all vehicles. For example, farm equipment and the township grader and plow could not cross the bridge. However, most of the farming operations were smaller-scale; their equipment could cross the bridge. One notable exception was Maine Township's new grader, whose bubble-gum light would not allow it to cross. Preservationist Joe Merz noted that, "It's difficult to stop a government project once it gets rolling. Sometimes one alienates those around them." Maine township supervisor Lowell Bjorgaard agreed, saying, "It's gotten to be quite a hassle."[12]

After nearly two years of effort on the part of the Water Street Bridge Preservation Society, they were rewarded with the news for which they had hoped. On 11 February 1981, news came that the U.S. Army, Corps of Engineers had denied the county's application to install culverts. The permit was denied due to the fact that culverts would have resulted in unnecessary expenditures, destroyed the historic bridge and character of the area, and threatened environmental quality and safety. While the bridge was still on the deficient list, environmental protection specialist for the Corps, Henrik Strandskor, highlighted the deciding factors: environmental assessment, including historical, aesthetics, recreational, economic, and environmental aspects.[13]

While the bridge was saved, repair work was desperately needed. However, this too was divisive, as the vote of township supervisors was not unanimous in seeking a grant for repair work, with Roberts voting no. This was not all that surprising, as sociologist Diane Barthel writes that preservationists "can never hope to rise above politics, to reach a point where all people share the same sense of what must be preserved…"[14] The Water Street Bridge Preservation Society applied on behalf of Maine Township for a grant from the Minnesota Historical Society, and was awarded $5,368 for bridge repair. Once the repairs were completed by a local company, volunteers from the township board, Water Street Bridge Preservation Society, and the Underwood Jaycees donated their time and labor to add a fresh coat of paint. And of course they celebrated with the ubiquitous potluck. [15]

There are a number of lessons that are to be learned from this micro-history. First of all, the Water Street Bridge Preservation Society demonstrated that it is possible to engage with government, at a variety of levels, and succeed. While it was no easy task, the group was able, after two years, to win a judgment in its favor. It took a prolonged effort, much research, and the willingness and ability to travel to meetings across the state, and articulately argue its case.

The effort also revealed the ability of many in the area to come together and forge a sense of community, even though they may have differed on a variety of political and social issues. The common interest at issue was preservation of a local and state landmark. The membership rolls of the Water Street Bridge Preservation Society reveal a diverse group who nonetheless had a shared interest in seeing the bridge saved, and they were able to set aside their differences and work together for a common good.

Saving Water Street Bridge was an important achievement. As historian David Glassberg has noted, "Historical and place consciousness are inextricably intertwined; we attach histories to places, and the environmental value we attach to a place comes largely through the memories and historical associations we have with it." No doubt many in the area had a strong attachment to the bridge, or had attached "a sense of place" to it, which is why many fought so hard to save it.[16]

Unbeknownst to members of the preservation movement at the time, in addition to saving Water Street Bridge, they may have saved others as well. According to author Roger Pinckney, "The lessons learned at the Water Street Bridge were applied several years later, to repair and preserve a truss bridge at Phelp's [sic] Mill."[17]

Despite having saved the bridge and preserved it as an historic landmark, nearly thirty years later, the county is at it again. As of this writing, Otter Tail County is accepting bids for replacement of Water Street Bridge. The past is always reinterpreted by new generations. Diane Barthel states that "collective memories are always selective"; therefore, an historic site is always "open to contestation."[18] What remains to be seen, however, is whether the call for preservation will be ignited again.

---

1   Diane Barthel, "Getting in Touch with History: The Role of Historic Preservation in Shaping Collective Memories," Qualitative Sociology 19, no. 3 (1996): 345.

2   Roger Pinckney, "Bridges of Otter Tail County," Pelican Rapids Press, May 21, 1997, 1-3.

3   Andy Leitch letter to Russell Fridley, Otter Tail County Historical Society Archives, Public Works Bridges (Misc.) Box.

4   Susan Halena, "Bridge replacement both lauded, criticized," Fergus Falls Daily Journal, December 20, 1979, 1; Otter Tail County Historical Society Archives, Public Works Bridges (Misc.) Folder.

5   Susan Halena, "Water Street Bridge backed during hearing," Fergus Falls Daily Journal," May 16, 1980; Otter Tail County Historical Society Archives, Water Street Bridge Preservation Society presentation to the U.S. Army, Corps of Engineers; Elizabeth Merz, e-mail to author.

6   Otter Tail County Historical Society Archives, Public Works Bridges
        (Misc.) Folder; Charles Carson, letter to U.S Army, Corps of Engineers,
        Otter Tail County Historical Society Archives, Water Street Bridge Pres-
        ervation Society presentation to the U.S. Army Corps of Engineers.

7   K.J. Peterson, "Minnesotans fight to save bridge," Fargo Forum, February
        4, 1980; In a 1977 ceremony at the Maine Presbyterian Church, the DNR
        designated that area of the river as the William O. Douglas Canoe Trail.

8   Susan Halena, "Water Street Bridge considered for national historic site
        listing," Fergus Falls Daily Journal, January 16, 1980, 1, 16.

9   Susan Halena, "Water Street Bridge on national list," Fergus Falls Daily
        Journal," May 15, 1980, 1, 10.

10   Andy Leitch letter to Russell Fridley, Otter Tail County Historical Soci-
        ety Archives, Public Works Bridges (Misc.) Folder; Russell Fridley letter
        to Andy Leitch, Otter Tail County Historical Society Archives, Public
        Works Bridges (Misc.) Folder; Susan Halena, "State-county group to ex-
        plore options for Water Street Bridge," Fergus Falls Daily Journal, April
        2, 1980, 1, 20.

11   Editorial, "Road and bridge fund ended '78 with deficit," Fergus Falls
        Daily Journal, September 28, 1979 and February 14, 1980.

12   Susan Halena, "Water Street Bridge backed during hearing," Fergus
        Falls Daily Journal," May 16, 1980, 1, 12; Otter Tail County Historical
        Society, Water Street Bridge Preservation Society presentation to the
        U.S. Army, Corps of Engineers.

13   Susan Halena, Fergus Falls Daily Journal, February 12, 1981, 1, 18.

14   Diane Barthel, "Getting in Touch with History," Qualitative Sociology: 362.

15   Pat Walkup, Fergus Falls Daily Journal, November 27, 1981, 1; Kathy
        Berdan, Fergus Falls Daily Journal, August 16, 1982, 1, 14.

16   David Glassberg, "Public History and the Study of Memory," The Pub-
        lic Historian," 18, no. 2 (1996): 17.

17   Roger Pinckney, "Bridges of Otter Tail County," Pelican Rapids Press,
        May 21, 1997, 1-3.

18   Diane Barthel, "Getting in Touch with History," Qualitative Sociology: 360.

Temporary Geography

by Bill Holm and Tim Rundquist

If enough snow falls, for a week or more,
the city plows and trucks pile it up in some
out-of-the-way place to wait
a quarter-year for it to melt.

Starter mountains appear on the flats:
the municipal lot grows a small Matterhorn,
over by First Lutheran, a stately Rainier,
the McKinley schoolyard, a whole Denali,
fifteen perpendicular feet, frozen solid.

On lucky days, when the road is plowed,
you can drive around town to admire them,
like a tourist discovering Svalbard—
   But be careful walking. You might slip and
   fall, and crack your body,
    to be transformed into geography,
    to disappear inside the lip of a new glacier.

PART TWO

It's Morning Again

by Robert Bly

It's morning again. Last night I spent hours
In a dream, and I had to keep silent,
As if we were visiting crickets or nuns.

It's a good morning. The cat sleeps all day
Under the lilac bush, and scholars go on
Discovering new maps of Constantinople.

My daughter has found that her girlish things
Were all moonshine. Now she has a baby.
She is the sun and the baby is asleep.

For Bridget

The Point

by Thomas R. Smith

In seventh grade, Carlene pivoted
in her chair to stab a newly sharpened
pencil into my left thigh just above
the kneecap, by design or in a violent
haste not to be seen by our teacher, Mr.
Collins, breaking off through the thick denim
of my jeans that finely honed graphite tip.
Maybe if I'd felt less ashamed of
the episode and told my parents they'd
have taken me to the doctor and he'd
have removed the embedded pencil tip.
But I didn't, they didn't, and he
didn't, and so to the present day when
undressing, I'll occasionally startle
as if seeing for the first time
the blue dot floating solitary,
tiny blue raft on the sea of pink
skin loosely over woven by dark
leg-hairs. That astonishment leads back
to thoughts of Carlene, whom I delighted
in teasing in that pre-sexual swamp, and
who at thirteen had perfected the ratted
big-hair of the greaser high school girls who rode

the backs of the local hoods' motorcycles.
Later, having outgrown my boyish rudeness,
I'd drop by her family's apartment
above the Labor Temple the spring we
graduated. It didn't seem to matter
that I was going steady with another girl.
Knowing I was college-bound that fall
made for a dizzy unattachment in which
everything certain lost its grip.
Even in seventh grade sitting behind
Carlene, daydreaming on the bouffant
dishwater dome of her hair, her slender
shoulder blades crossed by white bra straps
under her blouse, I must have admired
this girl, if not pretty, then spiky and alive
with rebellion, to have called down her
pencil's blue lightning to my flesh's ground,
to have taunted her with such reckless persistence,
literally beyond the breaking point.

A North Country Winter of Winters

by Lee Murdock

Having grown up in the north country, I have become accustomed to winter, but one in particular, the Winter of 1948-49, became the benchmark to which I have compared all others since.

The Snow Blower

With today's modern snow moving equipment, having a blocked farm road simply means the inconvenience of a couple of hours work with your tractor-mounted snow blower. During the harsh winters of the late 40s, however, before such extravagances became common, it often meant waiting days, even weeks, before the township V-plow could bull through and open up the road. If one was unlucky enough to live on a lightly traveled side road, the wait was always longer since you were low on the priority list and were the last to get plowed out.

In those days, the label "snow blower" was more closely associated with an Alberta Clipper than it was with a snow handling device. The most common snow handling device on farms then was a number 14 or 16 aluminum shovel that did double duty as a grain handler during harvest.

The ever-present potential of being blocked in and isolated for extended lengths of time earned forecasts of an approaching storm more than a passing interest from those of us who lived on remote farms. But, the weather forecasting Ouija board was even less accurate then than it is now, and storms often blew in unannounced.

Such was the case in mid-December of 1948, when an un-forecast Alberta Clipper howled through the area, leaving behind ten inches of new snow added to the several feet we already had. It piled in four-foot high drifts on the roads and hardened to near-cement consistency by sustained winds of 40 miles per hour. It blew all day and all night.

The Lost Chicken House

It wasn't until midmorning the next day that Dad felt it safe enough to go outside to do the chores of milking the cows, feeding them and the other animals and chickens.

Mom was surprised when he came back in half his usual time.

"Lois," he exclaimed, "the chicken house has disappeared!"

"What?" Mom asked. "The winds weren't that strong."

"Well, the only thing that's left is the very top of the roof," Dad exclaimed. With a twinkle in his eye, he went on to explain that the snow had piled up so high that it had completely covered the chicken house. The only evidence of its existence was the very top of its single slant roof peeking through the snow drifts.

After a hot cup of coffee to ward off the chill, Dad bundled up again and, with me by his side, set off to dig out the chicken house and free the entombed chickens. Although the initial discovery and response had been humorous, we knew that they couldn't remain buried too long, or they would run out of air or die of the concentrated ammonia fumes associated with chicken doings. We knew there was no use trying to dig out the entire house in snow that hard, so we busied ourselves with locating the door.

Fortunately the northwest wind had left enough space between the drifts and the south-facing front of the house to allow us to look down and locate the door. Then we proceeded to tunnel down, being careful to carve out steps in the hardened snow on the way, lest we reach the bottom and find ourselves without an escape route. When we reached the bottom we looked up to see the top of the snow drift some eight or more feet above us. We had been careful to make the spiral shaped staircase large enough so, when we reached the bottom, we had enough room to open the door. Then, not knowing what to expect, we hesitantly cracked the door and looked inside. What we saw was hens, all alive, as happy as fleas on a fat dog. There they sat in their own little insulated snow igloo, basking in their nests, in an almost tropical heat.

To us, the ammonia stench almost took our breath away and emptied our tear ducts, but it seemed not to bother them at all. Just to make sure, however, we propped the door open to let in fresh air as we went about the business of gathering the eggs and wrestling feed and water down the newly formed snow stairs. We ended up using that stairway for a good part of the rest of the winter until the spring melt finally exhumed the chicken house.

Frostbite Fears and The Chimney Fire

When we returned to the house chuckling over the fate of our entombed chickens, we were met with a sobering comment from Mom.

"Ray," she said, "did the fuel truck make it in to refill the fuel oil tank before the blizzard?" She had been at a ladies aid meeting the day before the blizzard, so had no way of knowing if it had. The ashen look on Dad's face was the answer. Without a comment Dad headed out the back door picking up the broken broom handle he used as a measuring stick as he went. He was back too soon.

"We've only got enough fuel oil left for a few more days. If, it doesn't get too cold. Of course, the colder it gets the more fuel we use. We'll have to turn down the fuel oil stove in the living room and keep the wood burner in the kitchen roaring to keep from getting frostbite."

Our dilapidated three-story house was so poorly insulated that we closed off the two top floors each winter and lived in the bottom 4 rooms. These were kept only marginally warm by the two stoves so we knew we were destined to be uncomfortable if the fuel oil ran out. Fortunately, we had cut a plentiful supply of wood for the old cast iron pot belly that inhabited the corner of our kitchen. The only unfortunate thing about the wood was it was mostly from cottonwood trees. Such wood that has only adequate heating potential and when burned in great quantities, leaves, among other things, a combustible layer of creosote in stove pipes and chimneys.

Blizzards are often followed by a cold snap, and such was the case this time. That, of course, meant our fuel oil supply was severely threatened.

With a large quantity of splittable wood piled high against the back shed entry, however, we felt uneasily safe—as long as the township plow made it through in the next couple of days.

It did not come.

Dad became increasingly concerned as the remaining fuel oil level dropped precipitously with each subzero night. The threat of running out of fuel oil meant that each night we stoked the old pot belly hotter and hotter. It would get so hot that when we turned out the lights it literally glowed red, and Dad could light his farmer's matches by just touching them to its surface. Running the old pot belly that hot for extended lengths of time was a prescription for disaster.

On the fourth night it happened.

We had just finished supper and Dad stepped over to the pot belly to light his after-supper cigarette, but, as he glanced up, he noticed that not only was the pot belly glowing, so was the stove pipe.

"Lois, we've got a chimney fire," he shouted.

With that, he lunged across the room, picked up the drinking water bucket and splashed it on the outside of the stove pipe. This wasn't enough to cool it down, however, and so, since we didn't have running water, we formed a snow bucket brigade from the nearest snow drift outside the back door. The whole process probably lasted only 10 minutes or so, but it seemed like an hour. When we were done the old pot bellied stove stood with an igloo of melting snow and ice surrounding it.

Roll Out the Barrel

That incident prompted Dad to act. He had already scouted out the road situation and found it was blocked solid, with 3 to 4 foot deep concrete-hard drifts for the entire half-mile to the main road. Assuming that such was the case throughout the entire township and county, he realized there was little probability of our lightly traveled road being plowed out soon. So he made the decision that, after chores the next day, he would walk the two miles to town. Now, a two mile walk in subzero temperatures is not a thing to take lightly. Mom tried to persuade him not to go. He was not to be deterred, however, and so, with a pair of sheepskin pants and coat over his long-johns and overalls and with three wool scarves wrapped around his face, he set off.

He had two choices for his path. He could walk the snow drifts and hope they were hard enough to hold his weight, so he wouldn't sink in and become entombed— or walk the railroad tracks which would add an extra half mile to his trek. He wisely chose the safety of the tracks, figuring the physical exertion would keep him warm. He arrived in town by late morning.

Once there, he arranged for the bulk dealer to meet him at the intersection of our road and the county road, which had been plowed, at

3 that afternoon. He still had a problem. How he could get the fuel oil the half mile from there to our house?

The answer to this quandary was an empty thirty gallon drum that had been used to store tractor gasoline. He had a container, but a remaining question was how to get it to and from the intersection.

Certainly he could simply roll the empty barrel that far. Rolling a 30 gallon barrel full of fuel oil back that far, however, would be an insurmountable task, and the drifts were too deep to make it through with the tractor.

With some trepidation, Mom reminded him of old Toby— the one remaining but retired workhorse that had, due to Dad's gentle heart, escaped the glue factory. Also resting among the discarded and antiquated farm implements was an old stone boat. This was a sled made with two four inch diameter fence posts as runners, held three feet apart with pieces of siding from an old demolished barn. Toby hadn't been harnessed for several years, but, with a bit of coaxing and much cajoling Dad managed to get him harnessed and attached to the stone boat. Then, with the thirty gallon barrel firmly tied to the sled, Dad, Toby, the sled, and the barrel set off across the tops of the snow drifts to meet the bulk truck.

An hour and a half later they were back with a full barrel of fuel oil. The results of his heroics warmed our hearts as well as our bodies for days.

But Toby was old, out of shape and failing, and the demands of plunging over and sometimes through the snow drifts had taken a toll on him—so much so, that Dad determined to only use him sparingly after that.

Food Bombs

Fuel oil was not the only commodity that ran short during that extended blocked-in period. Food supplies also ran low. As a typical farm family of the time, we weren't exactly in danger of starving. We had plenty of home-canned vegetables, and sauces, eggs, potatoes, milk, cream, and home-churned butter.

We had only a few packages of meat, however, which we had brought home from the locker plant. We kept it in our back porch entry way which, in winter, stayed so cold it doubled as a walk-in freezer. But we ran out of staples - not microwaveable meals or freeze pops or butter, but things that made the isolated life of a blocked in family more bearable-things like: sugar, flour, salt, baking powder, baking soda, and Vicks vapor-rub.

The lighter things Dad had carried back in an old grain sack when he made the long walk from town, but, the larger things, like a 20 pound bag of flour and the 5 lb. bag of sugar, were too much. No flour or sugar meant no bread, no donuts, no cookies, no pancakes, no home-cooked syrup and, worst of all, no mush!

When Dad mentioned this universal hardship of blocked-ins to my uncles, who ran the local Super Valu grocery store, it gave them an idea. They came up with a plan to help isolated farm families. For all I know, this may have been the first-ever home delivered grocery system in the state. It was rather unique. With today's technology, they could have taken the order by cell phone, filled it and then jumped on a snowmobile and barreled off across country to deliver the goods. In those late 40s, however, none of these things existed.

Consequently, there were several problems to overcome.

One was how to communicate with the isolated families, who didn't have telephones, to know what staples they needed. Two, how to deliver the groceries when all the roads were blocked. The delivery method was answered via the club that they both belonged to at the time. A group of men with a common interest in learning to fly had, a couple of years earlier, formed a flying club. By pooling their resources they had been able to buy a small, single engine Piper Cub and carve out a small grass airfield on the edge of town on land owned by one of the members.

My uncles got permission to use the plane to deliver the groceries.

Since they couldn't land, they'd pack the items in carefully cushioned sacks and drop them into a snow bank as they swooped low over a farmstead. These "Food Bombs" would then provide the necessary staples to the isolated family.

The vast snow banks also supplied the answer to the communications problem. If they hadn't heard from an isolated phoneless family in several days they would fly out to their farmstead, buzz it several times until they got the attention of the inhabitants, and then drop a note-wrapped rock asking them if they needed anything. Then, using the snow banks as easels and whatever leftover paint or spray cans , etc., they had, the blocked-ins would simply print what they needed in the snow.

The connection was made, the order was taken, and within a few hours (or at the very least by the next day), if the weather permitted flying, they would be the happy recipients of a Super Valu "Food Bomb"— payment due when they got plowed out and made it to town or the next spring, whichever came first.

Our family was one of the first to receive a Food Bomb after that December storm. It was not so much because we needed it badly, but rather we were used as a trial run since we lived closer to town and it was my uncles doing the bombing.

Dad had left an order for a sack of flour and a bag of sugar. The next day, as planned, my uncles flew over, buzzed the house and proceeded to drop the bomb. They had misjudged the hardness of the snow banks, however, and when the bag containing the flour and sugar hit, it split wide open, spewing a white cloudy mixture of flour and sugar into the air. Dad, who was standing just a few feet away from where it hit, became the first frosted snowman. Needless to say, they learned their lesson and future bombs were much better cushioned.

Free At Last

Opening the road after the December storm had been more of a problem than first thought. The township push plow found the wind hardened drifts impossible to penetrate, and so we had to wait for the country rotary plow. It seemed like we waited half the winter, but it was more like two weeks later when the county plow finally made its appearance.

Our isolation over, we felt much like prisoners who had been sprung from the state pen. Mom busied herself making up a shopping list while Dad and my sister and I worked on shoveling out our block long driveway to reach the newly opened road. By the time we got the driveway opened, it was after closing time for the stores so we decided to wait until morning to go into town.

Unfortunately, we had a minor wind storm that night and it blew the driveway and road closed again. This time, however, since the new drifts were only a foot or so deep, it was only a couple of days until we were plowed out again by the township plow. This time we made it to town and Dad treated us by taking us to the show, which was aptly titled "Ma and Pa Kettle Go to Town." As I recall, we had to wait for the second show because the first was sold out, but that was a minor thing after what we'd been through over the past weeks. Besides, it gave Mom and Dad a chance to visit with neighbors whom they hadn't seen in weeks and catch up on the local gossip.

The show was the high point of our trip to town, but, as we piled into our car while sharing a laugh over scenes from Ma and Pa, I managed to get my thumb slammed in the car door. And when we got home Mom discovered that she had forgotten to get the salt that had been high on her grocery list.

But, those incidents became the norm during that Winter of Winters.

Training Ground

by Stash Hempeck

My first classroom
was all hard lines and right angles—
pointed corners and razor edges
on rectangular steel tables,
on ladder-back wooden chairs
with square rungs and spindles.

I would sneak in
files—bastard and mill
for the metal-clad boundaries,
half-round and rat-tail for the wood,
and once even a small, smooth
triangular taper for
surreptitious work on the undersides .

Making little progress,
I barely managed to last the year,
and when my teachers realized
I couldn't be converted,
they gave me a ticket east
to the camps.

But luckily for me,
the train was late that night,
and in all the moonless confusion
I made good my escape.

A New York Junior High in the 1940s

by Evan B. Hazard

Junior high Assembly at Public School 3 was Wednesday at 9:00. P.S. 3 was on Grove Street, between Bedford and Hudson, in Manhattan's Greenwich Village. I had done grades 1-6 at P.S. 41, farther north in "the Village." But P.S. 41 ended at 6th grade, so I did grades 7-9 at P.S. 3.

P.S. 3 was five stories high. The first story housed the auditorium, a cavern that passed for a gym, and a lunchroom. Grades K-6 were on the second floor. The top three floors were junior high. Junior high had several sections of each grade; there were a few hundred of us. We used an entrance on Grove Street; K-6 kids used an entrance on Bedford, and their Assembly was at a different time from ours.

The principal was Miss Amy English. Nobody called her Amy, to her face. Amy exercised control by adopting a severe demeanor. So did some of her teachers, like Mrs. Casserly, the typing teacher, and Miss Palmer, a math teacher. Others, like Mrs. Betz, the librarian, Miss Graham (math), Mademoiselle McGillicuddy (guess), and Mrs. Kelly (English, and my 9th grade home room teacher) were friendly. They, of course, got better results. The male shop teachers were relatively easygoing.

Junior high was not a happy time. Amy required boys to wear white shirts and ties, and I didn't care for rules that serve no purpose. Most of you have never seen me wear a tie, and never will. When traveling, I carry a clip-on for emergencies. But ties were no big deal. The big deal in junior high is acceptance. I did well in most classes, was actually interested in most subjects, and generally knew the right answers. Teachers who liked anybody liked me. Therefore, a good many of my peers did not. I got along decently with some of the better students, but P.S. 3 had its share of thugs. I was not free of thugs until I got to high school, and then only at school.

There was also "released time" Thursday afternoons, starting when I was still at P.S. 41. We had to take a form home so parents who wanted to could sign us up for Thursday religious instruction at the church of their choice. Most of the thugs took release time, to little effect. My mother signed me up for St. Joseph's. Fortunately, most P.S. 3 thugs went to Our Lady of Pompeii.

In 8th grade released time, after three or four years of dull, repetitious, non-interactive, uninspiring dogma, I rebelled. I asked Mom to write a note releasing me from "released time," and she did. Amy English had me come to her office. Turns out she was of the same denomination, which, in a *public* school, should have been irrelevant. She was concerned that I not stray, but understood my impatience with instruction that was, in today's jargon, the "same old same old." She "suggested" that we acquire a suitable "story of the Bible," and that I read that.

So we bought "Hurlbutt's Story of the Bible," a substantial tome. Ironically, at St. Joseph's, instruction was in doctrine, not Bible. I had a catechism and a prayer book, but am not sure I had ever opened a Bible. I read well and loved to read, so got through Hurlbutt in a month or two. I don't remember having to report back.

Miss Holscher was a horse of another color. She was an eighth and ninth grade science teacher. Miss Holscher was certain, but often wrong. She seldom checked what she "knew" against observation. She told us that only introduced insects were harmful, and that, due to the sun's brightness, you cannot see the moon in the daytime.

You say, "Surely she was kidding, Evan; she was just trying to stimulate discussion." No, Miss Holscher didn't do discussion. She once used this true/false item: "The sun will last for eternity." She marked "true" correct. I objected that Sol would eventually stop shining. She said no: that since humans would no longer exist then, eternity would be over. Savvy pupils knew not to argue with ignorance cloaked in authority.

An Assembly before graduation in 1944 put the icing on the cake. Amy got it into her head to get serious with her charges about career choices. In Assembly, she asked what we planned to do with our lives. I don't remember what choices she gave the girls, but am sure they included not much more than secretary, teacher, and nurse. She gave the boys several choices; about half the boys' hands went up when she said "doctor" and about half went up when she said "mechanic." Few went up for lawyer or other trades. So she lectured us about our narrow outlook and unrealistic expectations.

My hand had not gone up for any of Amy's options; it would have had I known what was coming. Mrs. Kelly was sitting at the end of my row on the side aisle, behind the rest of the class. The seats between us were empty. She motioned me over. "Evan, you didn't raise your hand. What do you want to be?"

"A naturalist."

Mrs. Kelly stood up and announced to Miss English, and a few hundred junior high students, that she had a student whose career choice Amy had not listed.

Amy looked at me: "Evan, what do you want to be?"

I stood up and replied, to her and a few hundred junior high students, "A naturalist." I liked Mrs. Kelly, and didn't really dislike Amy. But these people had degrees in education. They once took child psychology, no? Did they really think this would edify the other kids? Did they not realize how embarrassed I would be?

How come I was free of thugs in high school? New York City's public school system had, and still has, what today are often called "magnet schools," as well as several specialized vocational high schools. One was Stuyvesant High School, at 345 East 15th Street, less than two miles from my home in the Village. It was a science-oriented high school for boys, and you had to pass a competitive exam to get in.

Because it was a pre-existing school that the Board of Education converted to a magnet school, boys from its immediate neighborhood could attend without taking the exam. Few did, and most of them soon transferred to other public high schools. There were few if any thugs at Stuyvesant. It was splendid preparation for college. It was a godsend.

Sweet Jesus Rolls

by Arnold Johanson

It all got dumped into the Fiesta Ware bowl,
the yellow one with the big white chip:
milk, flour, yeast, eggs, whatever.

She'd stir it up, set it in the sunlight
under a dampened dishtowel, wait for it to rise,
then go at it with her hands, squeezing

and beating, pounding the fates
that kept us all in small town parishes
so far from Minneapolis and home.

She sang hymns as she kneaded,
about Jesus our friend who wants us
for sunbeams. After it rose again

she tore off hunks of dough, caressed
them into shape, arranged them on sheets,
slid them in the oven, brought out, every time

the best damned rolls I ever tasted.
Sorry, Mom, I used a bad word.
But they were that good.

The Red Cottage on Jewett Lake

by Elizabeth Eriksson Sweder

The ritual of opening the cottage in the spring, after nearly six months of winter, was just as exciting as waiting for Christmas had been in December. We crossed the Red River into Minnesota, and chugged along Highway 52 from Fargo in our 1936 black Oldsmobile. Mother held the baby in the front seat, while we four older children scrunched together in the back, mounds of bedding piled around us. We nudged and jostled each other, jockeying for position as we watched impatiently out the windows, while mile after mile of flat, tar-black earth and tiny green shoots of freshly planted crops rolled by. The old car was known for its inability to reach any destination without a breakdown, but this time luck was with us.

With a war on, we were lucky to have any car at all. "Is this trip necessary?" Uncle Sam pointed his finger accusingly at us from a billboard along the way. "Yes! Yes!" we shouted. The trip seemed to take forever. Dad would have liked to drive faster, but the speed limit was only thirty-five miles an hour. If we drove slowly, we would save gas to help America win the war, as well as saving rationing stamps. We turned off the highway onto bumpy gravel roads, and left the flat prairie behind. As the terrain became hillier, we soared up and down over crests and valleys with stomach-flipping thrills, accompanied by shrieks of delight.

"When will we be there?" I asked for the umpteenth time. As the car climbed to the top of the highest hill, we came around the south side of the lake, and caught a glimpse of sparkling blue water beyond the pasture below. A chorus of shouts rose from the back seat, "I can see Jewett Lake!

I can see Jewett Lake!" "Last one in the water is a rotten egg!" "Race you to the beach!"

Shouts of "yea!" and "I'm getting out first," continued to erupt from the back, until at last Dad negotiated the car slowly downhill on a narrow, bumpy dirt road. Branches of maple trees brushed against the car and into the open windows, until we finally pulled up to the backdoor of the Red Cottage and stopped. We were moving to Jewett Lake for the entire summer, a time that would seem to last forever, and be repeated again and again throughout my childhood.

The Red Cottage, with a white painted wooden dragon running along the peak of the roof, its bright red wooden tongue flashing out at each end, was built by my Swedish grandfather, Leonard Eriksson, in 1923. He brought the plans back from Sweden, after a trip there to visit his parents.

The site of the Red Cottage on Jewett Lake was found by my paternal great-grandfather, James G. Shonts, who secured it for future generations of his family to enjoy; to him we owe our gratitude. He came to Otter Tail County from upstate New York in 1875, hoping to make money as a land speculator. The story goes that he arrived with $5000 in his pocket, and purchased 5000 acres of land for a dollar an acre. Part of that land was a farm at the southeast end of the lake. It stretched from the level, sandy south shore, suitable for pasture, for about a mile north. J.G. Shonts purchased the land from a widow who had filed a homestead claim on the quarter section, and failed to prove it up. In 1877, Grandpa Shonts, as my father called him, bought the farm for his family's use.

He chose a spot in the center of the east side of the lake for a camp site, where he and his wife Emma could picnic and play games, go fishing and swimming, and entertain their friends. Thirty years later, his daughter, Kate Shonts, married a young lawyer, Leonard Eriksson, who had immigrated to Minnesota from Sweden at the age of fourteen. When he arrived in America he did not speak English, but learned quickly, and made his own way in the world. In 1908, Leonard and Kate had a daughter, Sydney; two years later a son was born. They called him Jim, and he grew up to be my father.

The family's custom of spending the summer at Jewett Lake was well-established by Grandpa and Grandma Shonts, when in 1916, their daughter, Kate Shonts Eriksson, died. Leonard was left to bring up the children alone. The three of them continued to live with Leonard's in-laws in the Shonts family home, the "Clement House," in Fergus Falls, where Jim and Sydney developed a warm relationship with their grandparents. Leonard wanted to do everything he could to insure that his children had a happy childhood, and being at the lake was their greatest joy.

They spent their summers in a little stone house that Grandpa Shonts had built at the farmstead in 1878, a few hundred yards south of the campsite. Then, in 1920, he decided to retire and move to California. He sold the farm to a young bachelor, Albert Mobraten, but first made arrangements to plat the lakeshore along the east side of the lake into building lots. He named the development Forest Lodge. All the lots were to be sold except for the one in the middle that included the old camp site, which held so many happy memories for his family. That one acre lot was kept for future generations to enjoy. Three years later, Leonard decided that he wanted to build his own summer cottage right there, while his children were still young enough to enjoy it, before they grew up and left home. In 1923, he built the Swedish style summer cottage he had dreamed of. The wooden dragon across the peak of the roof would, according to Swedish legend, protect the family living there from harm.

The cottage was well-built, with vertical board and batten siding painted red. The inside walls were of half-log faced pine, with a matching vaulted ceiling in the living room. Prominently displayed at the gable end, opposite a fieldstone fireplace, was the head of a large buck deer, supporting an impressive set of antlers. The three small bedrooms had large casement windows that let in great drafts of fresh air. A glassed in porch across the front provided a clear view of the lake. All the outside walls were insulated with sawdust, making the cottage refreshingly cool in the summer, while snug and comfortable in the fall, when the family would drive out in their new automobile to enjoy the autumn colors.

That December, my father, then thirteen years old, and his sister Sydney, received a letter from their grandfather in California. It read:

Dear Grandchildren,

Enclosed find a Christmas present from your loving grandparents, being a deed to the Lake Shore cottage ground. I hope you will appreciate and enjoy the property and will keep it always. This one acre of ground will sell for as much money now as I paid for the whole quarter section forty-six years ago.

Should you be fortunate enough to acquire other lands, my advice to you is to hold it, hang on to it, keep it. Pay the taxes promptly, and

NEVER, NEVER, Mortgage it.

Wishing you a Merry Christmas and many of them, I am
Sincerely and affectionately yours,

J.G. Shonts

Leonard Eriksson still owned the cottage, but now his thirteen year old son and fifteen year old daughter owned the land.

Eighteen years later, my Dad, now a lawyer and a family man with a wife and three children, was still enjoying the bucolic tradition of lake-living. Working in his father's law office in the small town of Fergus Falls, where he had lived all his life, with the easy twelve mile drive back and forth to Jewett Lake each day during the summer, seemed natural and normal. The thought of living any other way or in any other place, had probably never occurred to him, or to my mother.

But when the Japanese attacked Pearl Harbor on December 7, 1941, whatever plans my parents might have had for the future suddenly vanished. Almost overnight, their lives, as well as millions of others, were uprooted. Thousands of families moved across the country. Legions of young men and women joined the military or went to work in factories that made munitions, tanks and airplanes. All across the nation, trains were crowded with uniformed soldiers. America would never be the same.

Dad's name was on a list of people who were designated to fill new government jobs, should the United States become actively involved in the war. A man from Minnesota, who was working in Washington, had asked the Dean of the University of Minnesota Law School to recommend someone with a sound legal background and excellent language skills for one of the new positions. Jim Eriksson, my dad, was that person. He was called to Washington immediately to work in the Office of Price Administration, popularly called the OPA. His job was to translate the new rationing laws, which Congress had already passed, from legal jargon into plain English that ordinary people could understand.

Dad left for Washington as soon as he could make the arrangements. Mother was expecting a baby; my brother John was born at St. Luke's hospital in Fergus Fall, Minnesota, on February 2, 1942, less than two months after Pearl Harbor. Because of a severe housing shortage in Washington, we were not able to join Dad for almost a year. As soon as he was able to find a place for us to live, Mother and the baby, Katherine and I, and our little brother Butch took the train to Washington, where Dad met us at the station. It was a joyful reunion for everyone.

My parents rented a small but comfortable old house with a wrap-around porch in Silver Spring, Maryland, a lovely old town dating back to before the Civil War. It was just at the northern border of the District of Columbia, enhanced by wide green lawns and towering shade trees. Through that summer and the next, we listened to southern accents as we played with the neighborhood children, changed schools again when we moved to a different house in a new development, tried to fit in, and endured the dreadfully hot, humid Maryland summers. Mother was pregnant again. On October 5, 1943, my sister Margaret was born. The Red Cottage was now only a dim memory.

One night at the dinner table a few months later, Dad said, "I've got some good news to tell you." This was cause to sit up and take notice, as Dad was a taciturn man, and said nothing unless it was important. "I've been transferred to Fargo, he said. "We're going to move as soon as we can get ready."

Mother clasped her hands together; raising them to her chest she said, "Oh Jim, that's wonderful! I won't have to go through another one of those terrible hot summers." She stood up, went over to my Dad's chair at the head of the table, and hugged him warmly.

"Fargo's only sixty miles from the cottage. It should be a pretty easy drive down there. The cottage would just be sitting empty. I'll see if I can find a car to buy when we get to Fargo," Dad commented. Looking back now, I can understand how much Dad must have relished the idea of moving back to the Midwest, and spending summers at the lake again. "Maybe I'll be able to go hunting next fall," he said.

It was that summer, when I turned eight years old, that I began to build the storehouse of memories that impressed Jewett Lake and the Red Cottage on my consciousness, helped shape my values, and established me forever rooted and grounded in Otter Tail County. It was drier than usual that June of 1944. The long neglected grass around the cottage was tall and unkempt, the old garden bordered with dead stems from last year's peonies, planted long ago by my great-grandmother. Stiff stalks sprouting bristly brown heads, the remains of last September's purple cone flowers and gaillardia, stood randomly about. A lilac hedge that separated the north edge of our property from the little stucco cottage next door, was bursting with fragrant purple blooms. Deep drifts of dried brown leaves gathered beneath the lilacs, and dogtooth violets peeked out among the grasses.

The Red Cottage was now twenty-one years old. Dad was a self-taught handyman who liked to putter around with projects on the weekends. He knew it would be easier for Mother, being there with five children, to have running water, so his first job was to put in a pumping system that would bring water from the lake for bathing, washing dishes, and watering the garden.

He found an old, used pump operated by a Briggs and Stratton gasoline engine, and a forty gallon water tank with a pressure gauge. He installed these at the bottom of the cement steps going down to the lake, along with sections of galvanized pipe connected together, starting from way out in the lake, to the pump and the tank, then up the steep bank to the yard, and across the grass to the garden. Pipes also came into the house through the kitchen wall, and into the sink. It was a profound relief not to have to carry water from the well for cooking and washing dishes. The older children were often called on to help when the forty gallons of water were gone. Mother would announce with mild alarm, "We're out of water!"

"Run down and start the pump," she would say to whoever was handy. It seemed to me that everyone else would scatter, and I would always be the one for the job. First I had to stomp down hard four or five times on a pedal that sparked the engine to life. It chugged and pounded with a steady beat, as a little red arrow advanced slowly around a glass dial to the number forty. Then I would take a sturdy stick I had previously garnered from the woods at the edge of the path, and use it to press down hard on a metal tab that caused the engine to shut down. I was fascinated by the thought of what might happen if I didn't stop the engine in time. Would the tank explode? Once I let it go until it reached fifty, before I lost my nerve and shut the engine off, perhaps averting a catastrophe.

Now that we had running water, there was little more we could do, in the way of improvements, without electricity. Roosevelt's "Rural Electrification Administration" (REA) mandated bringing electricity to all farms in the 1930's, during the Depression, but that program had been put on hold until the war was over. Summer cottages were at the very bottom of the list for getting electricity. We were fortunate, though, to have a telephone, left over from the 1920s. It was an old-fashioned hand crank model in a dark stained oak case, mounted on the wall in the back entry, sharing a party line with eighteen other families. It rang constantly, but we only answered if we heard our own ring, one long and three short jangling blasts. To make outgoing calls, we had to first call the operator, who would say, "I'll connect you." It wasn't until the sixties that we were able to get a modern telephone.

Our biggest fantasy was to have a new kitchen. That would have to wait a very long time, but the breakfast nook, built of the same dark stained pine as the log walls, was one thing that we didn't want to change. We ate all our meals there. It was crowded, but still roomy enough for the whole family to squeeze in and still include a guest or two. The children unlucky enough to be pinned against the end wall made their escape by crawling out under the table.

The trestle table had a long, flat stretcher about six inches above the floor, which enabled lively contests to place our feet on the stretcher in the best position to push a sibling's feet off. This resulted in a lot of sly but good natured pushing and nudging of feet, and complaints of "Hey, that's my spot. I was there first!" We played cards and board games— hearts, Rook, rummy, cribbage, or monopoly, in the breakfast nook on rainy days, and in the evenings after dark, with light from kerosene lamps.

Along one interior wall of the kitchen was a white painted cupboard that included a flour bin, a couple of small drawers, and shelves for dishes. On the three cupboard doors, Mother had painted a bright yellow dandelion, a sailboat, and a colorful sunfish. An old kerosene stove stood next to the sink, its four burners each with a little isinglass door that opened in order to light the wick. Water for washing dishes was heated on the stove in a large cast aluminum kettle.

The only work space in the room, a drop-down table made of yellow pine, was hinged to the wall under the kitchen window, propped up by a two by four cut at an angle, holding the table securely in place. On the little wall space that remained were placed two small cabinets that Mother had painted dark green, with colorful Swedish style flowers on the doors. The smaller one had an open shelf that held a pail of drinking water, carried fresh each morning from the well house, where a hand pump dispensed ice cold water tasting strongly of iron. Next to the drinking water, a nail had been pounded into the wall, upon which hung a long-handled aluminum dipper, conveniently located so that anyone could serve himself a nice cool drink of water.

We stored our milk and other perishable food in an enormous light blue, enameled icebox, standing importantly in the back entry. My dad brought the ice from the Hoot Lake Ice Company, where it had been stored in sawdust all winter after being cut from Hoot Lake in fifty pound blocks, then wrapped in burlap, transported home in the trunk of the car, and heaved into its special compartment with giant tongs that were kept hanging from a hook on the wall. During the hot, dry summers in the 1940s, slivers of ice, chipped off the big block with an ice pick, were a treat for the children, who competed to grab them from the floor before they could melt and vanish. There was no bathroom in the cottage, but an outhouse hidden discreetly behind the lilac bushes served the purpose, and bathing was accomplished in the lake, with a bar of soap.

My parents were very generous and inclusive with the use of the Red Cottage. Over the years, they invited countless friends, relatives, and sometimes people they barely knew, to visit or stay with us. In 1945, my Mother's younger sister Ruth had been divorced; her husband had left her for another woman. My parents invited Aunt Ruth and her two children, Ann, who was seven, and David, who was two and a half, to spend the summer with us at the lake. They arrived that June on the Empire Builder from Evanston, Illinois. We picked them up at the Great Northern Depot in Fergus Falls. Aunt Ruth was only in her twenties. She was thin and stylish, with fluffy, permanent-waved brown hair and red painted fingernails. She looked frail, tired, and sad, her face showing the strain of her divorce. With Ruth and her children, plus our family of seven, we were now a household of ten, crowded together in a small, three bedroom summer cottage, with no bathroom, no hot water, and no electricity.

The front porch, with two old army cots put in place, became sleeping space for my brothers Butch, who was now seven, and John, always called Joe-John, who was three and a half. He was a beautiful child with blond hair, rosy pink cheeks, and a round little mouth. He got the name "Joe-John" from a poem by A.A. Milne that Mother liked to recite:

Jonathan Joe has a mouth like an O,
And wheel barrow full of surprises.
If you ask for a bat, or something like that,
He has it whatever the size is.

Three year old David slept on a sofa in the living room. Margaret, whom we called Dee Dee, also age three, slept in the tiny bunk room, the very smallest of the bedrooms, which had built-in bunks on one wall. The top bunk was reserved for storing extra bedding and towels. That left the main bedroom, with a brass double bed for my parents, and the third bedroom for Aunt Ruth. Katherine, my cousin Ann and I were assigned to the guest cottage, our favorite place of all. It was a one room, unfinished frame building with a cement floor, which had originally been a garage. The large, screened windows were nothing more than rectangles cut out of the walls, with screening nailed over them. Heavy wooden shutters, hinged at the top and propped up with a pole, kept out the elements. We would let the shutters down only if it rained hard from the northwest, or stormed. It was almost like sleeping outside in a tent, with cool, fresh night air flowing freely through the screens.

We loved the excitement of summer thunder storms. First we would see faint lightning off in the distance, hear the soft, muffled rumble of far off thunder, and watch the storm as it moved closer through the roiling sky.

As the thunderheads advanced, we could sometimes see a white wall of rain moving toward us across the lake, then we'd hear the sudden roar of wind, lightning flashes would light up the whole sky, and tremendous thunderclaps seemed to shake the earth. We'd wait until the last few minutes before the rain hit, then run outside, drop the shutters, and dash back inside just as the first big drops of rain came pelting down. We'd listen to the sound of rain beating down on the roof, while we stayed dry, cozy, and safe inside. The best thing about the guest cottage, though, was that there were no adults within earshot; at bedtime, no one would tell us to be quiet and go to sleep. We would talk long into the night, laughing and telling stories, until we finally fell asleep.

One time when Dee Dee and her cousin David were around four, they snuck into the guest cottage to play with some matches they had taken from the kitchen. They didn't want to get caught doing something they knew they were not allowed to do, so they crawled under a bed to hide, and struck the matches on the cement floor. In a few minutes, the bedclothes caught fire, but they were quickly able to crawl out of their hiding place. David suddenly appeared at the Red Cottage, where Mother was making pancakes for the cluster of children waiting for breakfast, to report this latest trouble. He tugged at her skirt several times, murmuring "Aunt Lu, Aunt Lu," to which she replied, "Not now, David, I'm busy." He tried once more with: "Aunt Lu, the guest cottage is on fire!"

Aunt Ruth ran into the living room and looked out the window toward the guest cottage, calling out in her strong voice, "There's smoke pouring out of the guest cottage!" Mother quickly ran toward the little frame building. I had the presence of mind to grab the pail of drinking water from its shelf and follow her, running down the short path. When I arrived, she was backing out of the guest cottage, pulling a smoldering mattress through the door and into the yard. I got there just in time to throw the pail of water on the burning mattress, and the fire sizzled out.

A frequent visitor that summer was a friend of my father's, Pete Nelson, who had a degree in forestry and was the local County Agent. Pete, like my father, enjoyed fishing, camping, birds, nature, and all outdoor activities. He was a bachelor in his thirties who lived in Fergus Falls. He would come out to visit, get involved with my father's projects, and then get the kids involved too. One day Pete convinced Dad that we should all work together and build an outdoor fireplace out of the fieldstone rocks that were found everywhere. There were old rock piles at the edges of the surrounding farm fields, and in the woods that bordered the fields. For several days we all collected rocks and carried them to the yard. Dad always seemed to have parts of things around that might prove useful in some way, and he found an old iron grate that worked well for the cooking surface. With free labor, a lot of rocks, some cement and the iron grate, in a week or two we had a large outdoor fireplace that served us for many years.

We used it for cooking complete meals, as well as for roasting hotdogs and marshmallows. Pete even taught us children to bring the old enameled dish pan outside, fill the big tea kettle with water, and heat it on the fireplace grate. We didn't yet have a water heater, so it had to be heated on the stove. Somehow it was more fun to wash the dishes outside than in the kitchen.

When we were finished, we could throw the used dishwater into the tall grass by the sumac patch.

Pete, having studied forestry, was interested in anything having to do with trees. Dad owned a hundred and twenty acre wood lot in Friberg Township that he used for hunting, only about a mile from the cottage. He had acquired the wood lot during the depression years, when practically no one had any money, and the economy had nearly ground to a halt. The woodlot was part of a farm estate that my father was settling, and it needed to be sold in order to close the estate and disburse the assets to the heirs. They needed the little bit of money they had coming, but Dad couldn't find anyone to buy the woodlot, so finally he purchased it himself.

Over the seventy or so years since then, the woodlot has proved to be a wonderful resource. It was, and is, a beautiful stand of mixed hardwood forest with oak, maple, birch, basswood and poplar trees. Pete recommended that we harvest some of the wood to keep the forest healthy. Dad hired a man with a portable sawmill, which was set up in an open field across the road, and for a few weeks that summer, we children would go over to the wood lot and watch, while the tractor that powered a high-pitched, screaming saw turned out hundreds of board feet of oak and poplar lumber. The wood proved to be very valuable for our own use, and we got to play in the huge piles of sawdust.

One of the first building projects using the new lumber was a ten foot long, solid oak picnic table that stood near the outdoor fireplace for many years. Another one was replacing the old paperboard ceiling and interior walls in the kitchen with some of the poplar boards that had been milled into paneling. I remember getting up late one Saturday morning; Dad was there in the kitchen, ripping down the old ceiling while the breakfast dishes were still on the table in the breakfast nook. Chunks of torn paperboard, sawdust, old nails, wafts of dust and probably shreds of ancient mouse nests rained down on everything. Dad tended not to notice details like that. It was a mess for a couple of weeks, but eventually the kitchen had a beautiful new poplar paneled ceiling and walls.

The most memorable undertaking that my dad and Pete came up with, was building what might have been Otter Tail County's biggest, heaviest, most unwieldy home-made swimming raft ever, built over empty oil drums for flotation. The piece de resistance was an oak diving board mounted on the raft, special order from the woodlot. There happened to be one especially wide oak plank about ten feet long, that gave the men the idea for the diving board. They tapered it at one end to give it flexibility for some bounce, and covered it with an old piece of carpet to ward off slivers. Along one side of the raft was a bench complete with a back rest. Finally, a three horse Johnson outboard motor was attached at the end opposite from the diving board.

The little motor had just enough power to maneuver the raft out to deep water, where we anchored it in place. It was like "the little engine that could," just barely able to make it; but if a strong wind came up, both the motor and the anchor were useless, and sometimes we would end up almost a mile away on the north shore. Then we had to figure out a way to get ourselves and the raft back to our own beach. Storms that came up suddenly often ended just as fast. As soon as the wind died down, we started the motor and powered our way back to our own beach. But if the motor wouldn't start, we walked barefooted along the spring-filled shoreline, climbed a steep wooded bank, cut through Hess's farm, and hiked home along a narrow dirt road behind neighboring cottages. Later, we'd have to go back with adult help to either get the motor started, or tow the raft home with a fishing boat.

On the north shore of Jewett Lake in those days, where there is now a public boat ramp, there was nothing but deep sand, sparsely peppered with chokecherry trees, tufts of tall grass and weeds, and wild flowers. At the edge of the water, a sharp drop-off plunged steeply down into deep, clear water. We had been warned about the drop-off too many times to risk swimming there, although all of us siblings had learned to swim when we were young children. Despite the many hours we spent in the water, in boats or on the raft, we never wore life jackets, nor did anyone else we knew. We had hours of fun with the raft for many years, until it was finally reduced to firewood.

Late in the summer of 1945, Pete had come out to the cottage one weekend to go fishing with Dad. Out in the boat, Dad mentioned something to Pete about Ruth's hardship being alone with the children. Pete said, "You mean she's not married?" Dad confirmed that she was not.

"Why didn't you ever tell me that?" Pete asked. Evidently he had an eye for Aunt Ruth, but had kept his feelings discreetly to himself. A few days later, Pete asked her if she would like to go out for dinner with him. My parents joined them, and the two couples went to the Elks Club in Fergus Falls for dinner. Ruth was cautious about encouraging a relationship with anyone, but as they saw more of each other and had a good time, gradually they became close friends.

During the war years, it was important to have a "Victory Garden" to support the War Effort. My parents, always inveterate gardeners, had a large vegetable garden where they raised much of the food we ate all summer. Green beans and peppers, beets, potatoes, squash and cucumbers, carrots and tomatoes were mainstays of our diet. (We also had a constant supply of fresh fish.) Mother spent most of her time working in the garden, and on weekends she and Dad worked together. The children were required to pick beans, a chore I strongly disliked. We got fresh milk and eggs from a neighboring farm, and sometimes live chickens that my parents butchered themselves. In August, there would be corn on the cob. Mother baked bread and cinnamon rolls almost every week, made jams and jellies, and in the fall, they canned the bushels of tomatoes that we hadn't managed to eat fresh, as well as peaches. Home canned peaches were our dessert all winter.

Mother was permissive in many ways; on rainy days, she let the younger children build forts in the living room by turning the wicker furniture upside down and covering it with blankets. Then the younger children would crawl around inside the "rooms" they had created, while we older kids played cards or board games in the breakfast nook. We carved tunnels and rooms in the sumac patch at the edge of the yard, and made tents by attaching old World War I army blankets to the clothesline, the corners of the blankets weighted down with rocks, and quilts spread out on the grass inside the tent. There were only a few other children around, so we usually played with each other, and created our own entertainment.

When I was a child, there were only eight lots on the east side of the lake with cottages on them, all part of Forest Lodge. All the original cottages have long since been torn down, and replaced with new houses or cabins, except for the Red Cottage, which looks today just as it did in 1923.

I remember clearly the fourteenth of August, 1945, when Japan surrendered to the Allied Forces, and World War II came to an end. We celebrated in our own way, but our simple life at the Red Cottage went on as usual. When summer was over, Aunt Ruth and my cousins went home to Illinois. Ann carried a garter snake, secured in a hatbox, home with her on the train. The next year Aunt Ruth and the children returned to spend the summer with us again.

My brother Mark was born in August, 1946, at St. Luke's Hospital in Fergus Falls. With the war over, my father's job in Fargo ended, and in September we returned to Fergus Falls, where we moved into the Clement House on North Burlington, where my father grew up. He had inherited the house from his grandfather, J.G. Shonts, when he died in 1933. My father went to work for a law firm in Minneapolis, commuting home to Fergus Falls on the weekends; I started fifth grade, and with the war over and cars being built again, we bought a brand new, 1946 four-door Chevrolet.

In the summer of 1947, we returned once more to the Red Cottage. Aunt Ruth and the children joined us again, and life at Jewett Lake continued much as it had before. Even so, it was the end of an era. That summer, Pete was offered a job as a biologist with the U.S. Fish and Wildlife Service in Juneau, Alaska. In the fall, my parents sold the historic family home in

Fergus Falls, and we moved to Minneapolis. Ruth and Pete were married, and moved to Alaska at the end of the summer, in time for the children to start school that fall. In January, 1948, my youngest brother, Steven, was born in Minneapolis. He was the seventh and last child born to my parents.

After Pete and Ruth moved to Alaska, they continued to come to the Red Cottage with us for a few weeks each summer, for many years. Over the next few decades, the cottage was updated with electricity, and a new well brought fresh drinking water right into the kitchen. The bunk room became a bathroom, and a new modern kitchen makes life easier. The breakfast nook is gone, but the front porch became an eating area, with a commodious table that draws big groups of extended family and friends many times each season.

My siblings and I inherited the Red Cottage from our parents. The outside looks exactly the same today as it did in 1923, a landmark memorializing a way of life that has mostly disappeared, and that preserves our family heritage. Inside the cottage, a large, Victorian brass lamp with a hand-painted glass globe, which belonged to my great-grandparents, was converted from kerosene to electricity. It has hung from the ceiling in the living room for the past eighty-six years. Two of the comfortable old wicker chairs that were in the Red Cottage when I was a child, (used by my younger brothers to make forts,) and my parents' brass bed, are still in use.

When Albert Mobraten died in the 1950s, the farm he bought from my great-grandfather in 1920 was broken up. Eventually we were able to buy ten acres of woods and the grassy meadow across the dirt road from the cottage, where, when I was a child, Albert cut hay each June with his team of horses. Now my brother Steve keeps the meadow cut with a John Deere riding mower, and tends a vegetable garden and a softball diamond there. My sister Katherine bought nine acres of my Great-grandfather's farmstead, where she now lives. Her place includes the foundation of the little stone house that he built in 1878. My brothers Mark and Steve, as well as one nephew, have homes along the lakeshore that Grandpa Shonts platted as Forest Lodge in 1920, adjacent to the Red Cottage. The Eriksson siblings' grown children, grandchildren, and the first and second generation of nieces and nephews, cousins and second cousins, share in the use of the Red Cottage.

My husband, Don, and I moved to Otter Tail County from Minneapolis when he retired. We built our house on the northeast side of Jewett Lake, on part of the land where, for a short time in the 1870's, J.G. Shonts owned a farm. The values I learned during my childhood at Jewett Lake helped shape my character and have stayed with me all my life. I draw on the strength of those values every day. My parents lived the qualities of generosity and inclusiveness, of self-sufficiency, hard work, and family unity, which the Red Cottage represents. I hope it will stay in our family for many more years to come. In 2023, we will celebrate its one hundredth anniversary. I expect to be there. May everyone whose life has been touched in some way by the Red Cottage, be with us there in spirit.

The Silo

by Luke Anderson

Silage was chopped after first frost.
A full-blown silo stored feed for stock.
Cooked in a sweet-sour compost,
within walls of concrete block,
green-cut corn turned warm as toast.

Today, the tall tube stands hollow.
Storms have blown down the chute,
leaving door-holes in a vertical row
for winds to play tunes on the flute,
while thistles sway in the pit below.

The silo rises, useless and high.
Tearing it down is a huge expense
so it's left to poke at the sky.
Cattle no longer loaf in their pens
and the barnyard is dusty and dry.

Kids gone, Mom and Dad passed on,
the barn collapsed, boards decay.
Our farmstead, once alive at dawn,
sits silent, weathered and gray.
The silo looms like a tombstone.

The Window Washer

by Cheryl Weibye Wilke

Because I was enrolled in Photography 101 in 1976
    because I was young
because you were old
because you were sitting with the tools of your trade
    behind the glass of a vacant storefront window
because it was the frozen dead
    of winter in Fargo, North Dakota
because no one could see you, but you
    brushed my side through the pane
because I wondered whose windows you were waiting
    for spring to wash so that others could see
because you were old
because I was young, I stopped to take
    your photograph. Or was it merely
    an apparition exposed a ghost? I wonder now
because I am old
    I spend most of my time inside, polishing
    beautiful words, waiting for someone to see.

Return to District 176

by Vernal Lind

I approach the decaying building of my old country school: District 176, the Oakdale School, located in Leaf Mountain Township, south of Clitherall. Lilacs grow around the old pump. Oak trees are twice the size and height they were years ago. The playground is now filled with alfalfa, sweet clover, grass and weeds.

I walk forward to the crumbling cement steps with grass growing in the cracks. After hesitating a few moments, I try the door. It opens, and hinges creak. The empty cloak room smells musty, and the wainscoting is faded. A hallway leads me to the classroom, where I see broken windows, blackboards that have fallen down and a dirty floor with evidence that mice and other creatures have taken over the place.

A longing to go back to that simpler life comes to me. The world was different back in the 1940s during those school days. All at once, I am transported back to that time. The school house returns to what it was years ago, and the playground is filled with the laughter and talk of children.

In this spot we play "Prisoner's Base," "Captain, May I" and many other games. We never lack for games. My bat connects with the kitten ball (softball), and the ball goes past second base. A great accomplishment for a nine-year-old!

The pump. Other students and I pump water. We always do this task quickly so that we can get on with games. And in winter, this chore becomes the least favorite task.

I turn toward the lake and hills nearby. Down those hills and around the lake, my sisters and I walk or ski the mile to school each day. This wooded area invites us students to play and imagine all sorts of things. We think of Anne of Green Gables sitting in a secluded spot. We imagine discovering a cave the way Tom Sawyer did. And we tell ghost stories and talk about strange things, real or imagined, that have happened in the community.

The frame building becomes clean and white. The bell rings with that clear sound to summon me and my sisters to class. That bell had rung in the new twentieth century and invited my father and his brothers and sisters to this same school.

I enter the cloak room. Girls hang their coats and jackets on the right side; boys hang theirs on the left. The older students are privileged and hang their jackets closer to the door. The wainscoting is clean light yellow. By the other wall stands an old storage cabinet.

On the other side I see the water fountain. This fountain is an urn that holds two or three pails of water. We may not have the convenience of indoor plumbing and water, but we can push a button and water will come. The water not drunk goes into a slop pail. Nearby is a wash stand and a pail of water with a dipper. After trips to the toilet (also called the can) we wash our hands, but we have only cold water.

The opening exercises take place. We recite the "Pledge of Allegiance" and sing "America" and several other songs.

Classes begin. I am in fourth grade, sitting at my desk, working on an assignment. The roll-top teacher's desk is filled with books and papers. The teacher calls, "Seventh Grade Geography," and two students go up to the recitation desk. I work but I hear the older students talking about faraway places. The teacher pulls down a map from the map case and points to France and Germany, where a war is being fought. That world out there seems strange and wonderful, yet frightening.

Later, the teacher calls, "Third Grade arithmetic." Third grade problems seem so simple compared to the ones in fourth grade. I listen again to what I learned last year. In the back, an older student sits with a younger student, helping him with his assignment.

At noon we students hurry to have a drink of water and gather up lunch buckets or pails so that we can go outside for noon lunch—really a picnic. Actually, we have picnics every day the weather is cooperative.

The scene changes. A group of very wet children return from recess after playing in the late winter snow. We move our desks close to the floor heat register to warm up and dry out. Instead of regular classes, the teacher reads to us, and we cut out pictures. The smell of drying or almost burning mittens fills the room. The teacher reads to us. Our minds leave the classroom to visit faraway places and new people. There is a bigger, more exciting world out there.

The old clock on the wall tells me the time as well as the day of the month. Though I love my studies, I look forward to four o'clock when my sisters and I walk across the hills and fields to return to the warmth and safety of home. The ticking of the clock can be heard only during those brief periods when everyone is studying and the teacher has not called the next class. On the wall, the pictures of Lincoln and Washington make me think of life in an earlier time.

Some of the blackboards contain assignments, but others have our art work. By using various colors of chalk, we have drawn some country scenes. We worked hard on those during rainy days.

I leave the classroom and open a door to the library—my favorite place. This room with high ceilings couldn't have been more than four feet by eight feet in size. But this "best rural school library in Otter Tail County" brought students into a bigger world.

Books have that magic appeal. First comes Alcott's "Little Women" on the top shelf where the fiction shelf begins. Zolinger's "Widow O'Callahan's Boys" completes the fiction on the bottom shelf. The other half of the library contains fascinating books of history. Pre-historic times. Stories of great men and women. Then, there are those books about faraway places.

I visit this place as often as I can, losing myself in the world of books. I travel far. My world becomes much bigger than this limited physical world.

Reluctantly, I leave the library. As I walk through the classroom, I see the oak tree closest to the school. I return to the cloakroom and decide to exit the side door. As I stand before the side door, I remember the stairway to the basement. That basement looks mysterious and forbidding. I wonder what creatures may have entered this dark place. We usually avoid this place for fear of little black and white animals.

One time we clean up and work in the basement. It is Halloween. We are making the basement into a haunted house. The arrangement of old desks and curtains suggest secret passages. Wet macaroni is used for brains of the dead. Other slimy objects suggest whatever a child can imagine. The night is damp and rainy. We have all the excitement and mystery of the season. Extra guests make the night more special. And we have Halloween treats.

The side door takes me into an area near the boys' and girls' toilets. We boys are forbidden to play near the girls' outhouse. However, I see one or two times when the tag games got out of hand—and the girls would retreat to safety. The convenience of indoor plumbing would not come to the farm homes of this area for at least another ten years.

In winter we leave the school to go to the lake and play on the ice. We don't have skates.

Overshoes work well on warm days. We slide down the hills. And we play versions of fox and geese. What exhilarating winter fun!

I turn the other direction and see hilly fields and pastures. In spring and fall, we hunt gophers.

We use bats and carry pails of water to get the creatures out of their holes. We cut off the tail or back legs for bounty. We feel excitement as the bounty money goes into our club treasury. We will have money for treats or something special.

I see that steep hill. In winter, I see us skiing and building a ski jump. I see myself, trying the jump for the first time.

My mind moves through those eight years. Faces of schoolmates pass before me. I see myself changing from a frightened, very small first grader to an eighth grader. Those eight years fast-forward.

I walk around the yard. Each tree evokes memories. Each spot includes a scene where something happened. Even the flag pole has its memories. I see the flag at half mast. Death claimed Franklin D. Roosevelt. I feel the sadness as we mourn the President.

I smell that dry dust. Voices echo. There is laughter and excitement.

I look up to the old bell tower. The bell, no longer there, must have rung for seventy or eighty years. It summoned me. It summoned my father and his brothers and sisters. It summoned a whole community. That bell rang in the new century.

I enter the building once more. I hear the familiar songs. "America the Beautiful." "There's Music in the Air." Other songs.

I leave the sounds of music. I leave a way of life. I have learned to face life with curiosity and imagination and hope and faith.

I take out my camera. One last picture.

Author's Note: Shortly after I wrote this memory, the local fire department conducted a controlled burn. Part of the foundation and some rubble remain.

Landmarks of Memory

by Jeanne Everhart

Where are the landmarks—
old buildings, wood bridges,
the old oak tree, or pasture fence
that helped me get my bearings?

Clouds, gray skies and dark nights confound
my sense of North, South, West and East.
Familiar houses are painted unfamiliar colors,
or they have new siding, or are gone like
the old barns with sagging roofs
overtaken by weather and time.

There are still a few old landmarks
to point me in the direction
I need to take from here to there.
Rush Lake, Otter Tail and Leaf Lakes
are like old friends that I can count on.

Deer Creek, the hometown
of my youth, exists only in memory.
The Fire Hall still marks the corner
although it is now a museum.
There is no Old Home Place

to come back to, and the lot
where the house and garden were
looks so small now, but black walnut trees
Mama planted years ago have grown.

You would think at least one brick
would remain from Hoyts Hardware
that is now gone, along with
Elmer Dahl's beer joint and his
five cent, two scoop ice cream cones,
the Corner Cafe where can-cans swirled
over jitterbugging feet, in front of the jukebox,
Thorpes grocery store, Katzke's Butcher Shop
with Kay and Butch smiling greetings
when we walked to the counter
across squeaky uneven wooden floors.

Oscar Lindblom's Barber Shop
is only a memory of me
holding my screaming brother
on my lap, for his first haircut.

The urge to return to childhood places
stirs us with yearning for youthful faces, or
longing for family summer picnics
on a wildflower lined riverbank,
cows nearby cooling in the river, while we
cast line from homemade willow fishing poles
or maybe cool ourselves in the cattle crossing.

Memory is the best place to visit childhood.
Empty rooms and pastures do not exist there—
Our horse Beauty still runs and grazes on green grass,
our old house still stands, and I jump from my feather tick
then race downstairs to warm by the stove on winter mornings;
music of Daddy's fiddle and Mama's guitar float
in the air filled with love, voices and children's laughter.

All the faces of friends and family are alive in memory—
as are marshes with blackbird songs, milkweed patches
for contemplating the monarch caterpillar,

the train whistle signaling time to go to the post office.
My rat terrier Tiny, chases the black furry rag I drag,
nipping at my ankles in play.

How do you come home with no home to come to
or recognizable landmark to guide footsteps?
Whose feet are these that shuffle and falter?
I close my eyes and once again they run barefoot
in plowed furrows, behind Daddy and the horse.
Memories are everlasting autobiographies
holding tightly to landmarks of time.

Don't Leave Your Flat Screen TV in Your Fish House

By James Bettendorf

It's January, and thieves are raiding fish houses
on Lake Minnetonka, stealing anything they can
from these temporary cabins on ice, especially
computers, video equipment and TVs.

They snatched our cooler, empty of course,
but we intended to fill it this trip
so our beer would not freeze. They didn't take
the paisley couch, exiled from our basement.

Leading away from our gray canvas shelter, footprints
are wind-swept to oblivion before reaching the wooded
shore. The burglar may have glanced up to see the brilliant,
red and green sweep of northern lights.

PART THREE

For Sharon on Her Birthday

by Thomas R. Smith

That summer we set out to ride the rails
to pick apples in Wenatchee,
the Twin Cities yard bulls, unlike their more
tolerant western counterparts, weren't
having any of this romance of the railroad.
Like Bob Dylan, we ended up out on Highway 61.

Today I'd call it hopeless, the two of us,
our oversize backpacks, and your husky,
Jubal, whose head was so large I imagined
genius canine ideation going on
inside its furry rotunda. But in those days
it was possible—and it happened—that
someone would stop to shoehorn our whole crew
into a VW bug and that we'd make as good
time as if we were driving ourselves,
such was our nonchalant good luck. And that
was only the prelude to escapades
in a migrant world now lost to us both,
though scenes from that light-drenched Washington
landscape still play in vivid rotation
on my mental slide-carousel.

And you, friend,
dauntless hitchhiker of old, your taste
for adventure has served you well in living
so that the years have never become
the bars of a caged existence but instead
stored-up cells of some honey of sun
and wind preserving the sweet taste of
our twenties' free roads and hippie skies.

Squaw Candy

by Tim Rundquist

like the mississippi, the amazon, the congo, all rivers of the imagination,
the yukon has its own distinctive cast of fellow-travelers: the steam-driven
paddlewheelers, chanting "wood, wood, wood" as they growled upriver
a modern-day variation, fueled by the endless ingenuity of the alaskan busher:
an old jeep straddling a raft, paddles appended to tires, hop in and drive downcurrent; canoes, skiffs, logjams
    and every other watercraft imaginable

    in the winters, the frozen river is a highway for dogsleds, snowmachines,
    bushplanes-on-skis, pickups with studded tires; even antique bicycle, pedaled
    all the way downriver from dawson by someone escaping the klondike gold
    rush, bound for the beaches of nome: pausing in eagle for lifewarming cup-of-
    joe then thanks, i'll be leaving now and off he went, pedaling frozen balloon-
        tires over clear pack-ice and hardcrusted snowdrifts

springtime sees the railroad-car ice floes, creaking and groaning in
switchyards until bursting in downriver runaway-stampede:
for this rare time, they have the river surface to themselves
but below the chaos lurk the most noble fellow-travelers: the salmon
kings and reds, pinks, coho and chum, arriving first by ones and twos
then
filling every channel and backwater in heroic numbers, a silent city
to the
     scattered souls on the shore who set their calendars by the arrival

     just upriver from eagle, we see the first wooden fishwheel: perched
     on the
     riverbank, driven by current, perpetually in motion: a zen ferris-
     wheel
     we watch as a silvery form is scooped from the current, is lifted
     to the apex of
     the carnival then delivered sliding and thrashing to the gathering
     basket: to be dried, cached, grilled over campfire coals; to become
     thick
     salmon-steak on dinnerplate, midwinter dogteam fuel
          or even squaw-candy

the athabaskans and other people of the river make a special salmon-
jerky:
sliced long and thin, salted down, sweetened and slowly smoked; the
aroma
of the smoker makes the bears dream in technicolor and the end-result
is squaw-
candy: tough, sweet, chewy, essential; to be enjoyed while splitting the
wood,
walking the trapline, feeding the dogs, watching the
     big river go by between raised porchrail feet

     the natives who still run the riverside fishcamps always have plenty
     of
     squaw-candy to offer: some come in canoes, some in guttural-
     voiced
     motorboats to meet us mid-current; they tie up alongside like
     benevolent

pirate-skiffs, long bandoleers of salmon-jerky draped over shoulders:

only a buck a rope

the people of the river circulate among my guests, offering rough handshakes

and ready smiles; they quickly dispense their produce and are off again,

pointing their bows down the sunflecked current

and my guests, tasting the squaw-candy, are tasting the rich

lifeblood of the interior country

savoring my own strip, legs on the boat railing, i watch a moose swim across

the yukon, not too far downriver: massive head and shoulders well above

the waterline; just off the stern, a tangle of driftwood, torn by breakup-ice

from some unnamed tributary, speeds by: bound for the bering seashore,

to become fuelwood for the coastal yupik;

a gift from a forest they can scarcely imagine

Moles

by Sybil Baker

Although Diane and I might have toughed it out for a few more years, leveraged the fighting for sex, love, human contact, or whatever you might call it, we both agreed I should move out for the sake of the boy. So I packed all my stuff into a cardboard box while the kid was at school, and my new landlord Paul picked me up in a truck with more rust than body. We drove about ten minutes to the other side of town, or what passes for town in South Dakota. He pulled up to a ramshackle two-story house surrounded by a yard pockmarked by hundreds of mole holes.

"Welcome to paradise," Paul said. His hand snaked into an opening beneath the floor boards and shut off the truck.

I should have known that the rental ad in the paper was too good to be true: Roommate needed for spacious country home a few miles from downtown. Tinted plate-glass window in bathroom. Spectacular views. Tiled roofs. Wood burning stove. Fresh spring water. Sauna. $100 a month. The sauna did me in. I pictured myself steaming away my aches and pains after my night shifts at the convenience store three days a week.

Paul gave me a tour of the grounds, as he called them, saving the sauna for last. The bathroom did have a tinted plate-glass window with views of the neighboring field, which I later learned was the natural supplier of the weed-grass Paul smoked. What he didn't mention was that the bathroom was an outhouse shed in the backyard. The roof on the house, or most of it, was tiled as advertised—with plastic lunch trays. The rustic wood-burning stove was the only heat for the house, which meant that my bedroom upstairs would be an icebox in the approaching winter months. The fresh spring water, from a cistern out in the back, was our sole water source. And finally, there was indeed something that passed for a sauna—a shack with a few rocks piled up in the center under a stack of wood for the fire. After he showed me how to light the fire and ladle water on the rocks to generate steam, he invited me to smoke grass with him in the sauna, but I declined. I wasn't ready for that kind of intimacy yet.

The first night I learned about another omission in the ad—the interminable scratching on the other side of my bedroom's plywood wall. I lay awake listening to the creatures running back and forth, certain they would eat me alive if I fell asleep. After tossing and turning for what felt like hours, I padded downstairs to the main room to have it out with Paul.

He was sitting on a stool in front of the stove, barefoot, in torn jeans and a t-shirt finger-painted in soot. His greasy hair was bundled with twine, like a pile of twigs. Paul lit the tip of a rolled-up newspaper from the wood-burning stove. He watched half the paper burn to ash before he reluctantly tossed it into the flames. The room stank of rotten eggs and sour milk.

"What's behind the wall?" I spoke through my hand, which was covering my mouth and nose to temper the odor.

Paul squinted at me, as if he were trying to remember who I was and why I was in his house. "Ah, just some field mice. Harmless things." He brushed the ash from the front of his shirt with his oil-stained hands as he stretched his long skinny legs out from the stool toward me.

The stench, I realized, was Paul's feet. The closer his feet got, the more I had to back off. "Well, I think you should get rid of them."

Paul grunted noncommittally. He pulled his feet up to the stool and turned back to the newspaper spread out in front of him. He grabbed another sheet and rolled it tight. He lit the edges again and waited for them to burn halfway, like he was preparing a sacrifice before he fed the remains to the fire.

"This isn't over," I said, feeling foolish as soon as the words were out of my mouth. Desperate to escape his feet, I trudged back upstairs to bed, wishing for a blanket, or better yet, Diana, to keep me warm. But, as the night wore on, I became certain the scratching was not being made by field mice. The trap I laid the next morning outside a pile of trash under my bedroom window confirmed my suspicions. I showed Paul the rat, the trap cutting it at the neck, a heavy dark brown lump as large as kitten. He nodded and rubbed the stubble on his chin. His pockmarked face turned from the trash pile to the dead rat, as if he were still trying to make the connection.

"Only one option here," he said. "Gotta burn 'em out."

Later that afternoon, as the sun was beginning to set, Paul and I placed a few tins of milk and tuna near the trash pile. When we had about half a dozen stray cats licking the remains of the cans, Paul lit the cones of the newspapers we held to set the trash on fire. It only took a few minutes for the rats to start crawling out, and soon, the ground was a moving blanket of gray.

Like most creatures in South Dakota, the cats, unaccustomed to good fortune, were overwhelmed by their sudden booty. At first they froze like statues, unable to act. Then, almost collectively, they pounced on the rats, hardly tasting the blood of one before they moved on to another. Their kills barely made a dent in the exodus, though, as the gray cloud dispersed toward the nearby field.

It was all good fun, but after I helped Paul douse the fire with water from the cistern, it was time for me to get ready for my shift at the convenience store. I had given Diana my car, an old Chevy Nova, so now the only transportation I had was my feet. I allotted two hours for the five-mile walk to the shop on the other side of town, which was nearer to where Diana lived.

The sunrise walk home from the convenience store was therapeutic. I saw all kinds of things that I hadn't before: deer grazing quietly, wild coyote searching for prey, a few heron at a watering hole, all tinted an orangey pink from the rising sun. I began looking forward to that time, so sacred and without concern for my own screwed-up life, that I was actually able to think about things that I normally couldn't. I tried to figure out what had happened between me and Diana. Unfortunately, no matter what angle I took, I couldn't see us getting back together. Like a country song, we fought too much, loved too little. Not good for me, for her, and especially for the boy.

When I'd get home, the sky was more blue than pink. In the sauna, I'd light the fire and splash water on the heated rocks until the shed was so steamed up I couldn't see my hands in front of my face. I'd work up a good sweat before rinsing off with the cold water from the cistern. Then I'd walk upstairs, close the curtains so that the room was reasonably dark, and fall asleep before Paul even woke up.

Then the weekend arrived. Friday didn't start off too bad. Paul came home from his job at about six. He worked at the university in building and grounds maintenance, an irony that he never seemed to appreciate, given the condition of his own place. I joined him for a sauna that evening, and afterward we sat in the yard in the beat-up lounge chairs smoking grass, celebrating the start of the weekend. The back lawn was a miniature minefield, a wave of tunnels that the moles had dug. As the stars popped open across the expansive sky, Paul, emboldened by our success with the rats, declared that the moles would be the next to be evicted starting tomorrow.

I had four days off and was looking forward to sleeping nights. That night was the first one in my bed since we'd burned the trash pile as I'd been sleeping days. It was also the first chilly night, one that foretold a long winter in that unheated room. I vowed to buy a heavy blanket with my next paycheck, even if it meant living on bread for a week. In the meantime, I removed the tattered curtain from the window and cocooned myself in it. I closed my eyes, waiting for delicious sleep. Then I heard the scratching again. "Damn," I mumbled. While we'd gotten rid of the rats in the trash pile, the ones who lived within the walls of the house were there to stay.

They were like industrious ants. Real night owls. Scampering from side to side, copulating, nesting, and gorging. They reminded me of the way it had been with me and Diane, during the good times. Now listening to all that busyness wore me out. I finally fell asleep in the early morning, just as the rats were settling down. When I woke up, it was high noon, and the autumn sun burned my eyes through the curtainless window.

If I had assumed that Paul might spend his weekends on the million and one home and yard repairs the house needed, I was soon rid of that notion. I found him reclining in the lawn chair in the back yard with a stack of newspapers on his lap. A joint was clenched between his lips so his hands were free to roll the newspapers. He rolled the newspapers with the expertise of a joint smoker, even and tight, the ends straight. As soon as the paper was rolled, he struck a match and relit his doobie before lighting the paper and stuffing it into one of the holes near him. Paul nodded in satisfaction as the smoke emerged from the other end of the mole tunnel. Removing the grass weed from his lips, he exhaled smoke rings, like an executive with a cigar.

"What's up?" I asked, trying to sound casual.

"Smoking the moles out." He eased himself back into his chair to roll another newspaper. He asked me if I wanted to join in on the festivities, but I declined, telling him I didn't have the same affinity for fire.

Instead, I walked the hour into town, figuring I'd check out a book from the library, a thriller or mystery, then cross the street to the coffee shop, which offered free refills. And that's what I did. Except that just after I'd taken my first sip of coffee and was folding back the well-worn cover of Steven King's The Stand, I looked out the large glass window to Ned's bar across the street. Diane was walking in with a man who looked even scruffier than Paul. He was a biker-type, with large shapeless arms sticking out of a sleeveless denim jacket. He wore beat-up boots, had thick black hair bunched in a ponytail, and from what I could make out, sported a tattoo that looked like a skull on the very hand that was scooping Diane's ass.

It had only been a week, and she was already with someone else. Or, maybe, she'd been with the guy for longer. I tossed the novel in the trash, which would later result in a $33.35 lost book and overdue fine for a $4.99 paperback, but as was often my case back then, I dealt with the consequences later, if at all.

I strode across the street to the bar and pushed open the door, ready to have my ass kicked. Diane and her new man were sitting at the bar, laughing, as the barman deposited two large mugs, fresh and foamy, in front of them. Then the burly biker lit her cigarette, like he was Frank Sinatra, and my heart just broke. I was about to turn and leave when she saw me.

"Barry!" By the way she stood up I could tell the beer at the bar was not her first drink of the day. She half ran, half stumbled toward me with open arms. She pulled me into a bear hug, like I was some long lost brother back from the war, and not her live-in boyfriend of two years and three months until last week.

I didn't return the hug, not out of malice, but because suddenly every bone and joint ached so much I couldn't move. The biker guy raised his mug half-heartedly in my direction. I ignored him.

Except for the fact that her happiness gave her a momentary radiance, Diane did not look great. Her unwashed hair was haphazardly secured with a few barrettes. Her ashen face told me she'd been smoking and drinking a lot. She had the soft malleable thinness of someone who was out of shape and not, as my mother would say, eating her vegetables. Her eyes were a temporary dark blue, not their usual watery grey.

"Where's the kid?" I managed finally. I hadn't moved from the door.

"At home," she said, smiling wide and lopsided.

"By himself?"

"None of your business," the biker guy said from his stool.

"The hell it isn't." I pushed Diane aside and lunged for him. He batted me away with his free hand so that I reeled back into Diane. Next thing I knew, the bartender had me cuffed by my jacket and was shoving me out the door. He watched me from the door, yelling for me to go. Through the window, I saw Diane sitting on the biker's lap kissing him, her hands occupied with her beer and cigarette, indifferent to the pain she was causing me, and the biker, too, not now, but someday, and probably her son as well. Oblivious in that way people are when they are in love. My limbs melted and whatever fight I'd had a minute ago was gone.

That night I lay in bed, drunk from the bottle of Scotch I'd picked up at the liquor store and finished on my way home. Rolled up in the curtain like one of Paul's doobies, I was fortunate enough to pass out before the rats began their party. A few hours later, I woke up from a dream that Diane was throwing a bucket of water on my face, but it was just the roof leaking.

Above me, a sudden rainstorm had managed its way through the only part of the house not covered with trays. Drunk, wet, and groggy, I stumbled down the stairs and curled up next to the wood stove. I fell asleep, warm and dry, but by morning my body ached from sleeping on the floor. I couldn't move my neck in either direction, and my lower back was as stiff as a nail. I limped to Paul's darkened room and rolled him awake.

"What's up?" he said, congenially.

"There's a goddamn leak in the roof above my bedroom."

He blinked a few times before he recognized me, and I realized his greeting had come from some dream he was still inhabiting.

"Ahh…no trays there." He scratched his head. "Lost my job at the elementary school before I could get enough to finish that part."

"How about if I just take some trays from here to finish then?" I pointed to the ceiling above him.

"Can't do that." Paul was sitting up now. His feet stank up the whole room. "It's like a house of cards. Remove one and the whole thing goes."

"I can't sleep there."

"Take this room."

"No thanks." I didn't think I'd survive the stench.

"Well then, you can always get more trays." He closed his eyes and turned from me, banishing me from his room.

That was how I ended up walking the three miles to the elementary school Monday morning. I arrived just as planned, in time for the first lunch shift. The trick was to look natural. I'd hoped to blend in somehow, pass myself off as one of the maintenance men, and so I just sauntered into the cafeteria as if it were the most normal thing in the world, like a twenty-seven-year-old-guy with a beard and flannel shirt and work boots and jacket patched up with duct tape belonged there.

Although I was the only adult in the meal line, no one seemed concerned. I briefly considered taking a dozen trays from the stack and walking out then and there while mumbling something about tray repairs, but in the end I thought it too risky. Besides, I was hungry. I picked up two stacked trays, and waited as the cafeteria ladies ladled the food of the day on a plate: Salisbury steak, mashed potatoes, and pudding. Not much had changed from my own school days. I paid the cashier, who didn't even glance at me, but as soon as I emerged from the lunch line, I was busted.

The cafeteria lady shouted at me and waved from her station near the microphone she used to keep order. When I ignored her, she rushed toward me, her tennis shoes squeaking as they unstuck themselves from the various food and drink long dried on the floor.

"You must be here to see Joel," she said, panting. When she breathed out, I caught the stale smell of alcohol. A flick of red lipstick stuck on her front tooth.

"I was going to have lunch with him." I'd forgotten the whole school kind of knew me since I used to take the kid here and pick him up on my days off. I even went to a parent-teacher conference once when Diane was working.

"He's sitting over there."

He was by himself at the end of the table with his tray of food that was mostly paid for by various government programs. I wasn't sure if he ate alone or if his friends had not yet gotten through the line although I suspected the former. I sat in the chair opposite him, tray to tray. He looked up and nodded, like he wasn't surprised to see me there at all. Then he went back to cutting his steak. He was a good-looking kid: his olive complexion and deep dark eyes came from his father, a local Diane had met while on an extended vacation in Mexico. A two-week stand. A man out of the picture before he'd even been in it.

"How's school?" I cut my own steak and put a big piece with some mashed potatoes in my mouth. Half the lunch was gone in that one bite.

"It's all right." He opened his milk carton and dropped the tiny plastic straw in it.

"And home?"

He looked me in the eye then. "The same." He sucked his milk.

The same. That statement could have meant anything, that he was lying about motorcycle guy to protect me, or he didn't know about him, or that, and this one hurt just a little, that the biker was just another new guy in his mom's life, no different from me. I decided not to press. Instead I opened my milk and swigged it. "Hey, I'm going to come and visit you everyday for lunch this week. Is that okay?"

He nodded with the sad indifference of one who has learned at an early age to not get too worked up about things. I hated involving the kid in petty theft. Even though the cards were stacked against him, I still hoped he'd turn out all right. But my own tiredness, sore neck, and the threat of rain later in the week overtook my concern for the kid's moral development.

"And one more thing." I turned around to make sure the cafeteria lady wasn't hovering and was immediately reminded of the neck pain from sleeping on the floor the night before. "Can I have your tray?"

All that week the boy never asked me why I wanted the trays. He just compliantly gave his to me after he'd dumped his food and milk carton in the trash. I knew without asking him to that he would not tell his mother. And that was how by Friday I had enough trays to finish tiling the roof as well as a few spares, for emergencies or—Paul's idea—winter tobogganing.

Life improved for a while. I adjusted to a life without hot water and a flush toilet. My roof was fixed. The rats and I came to an uneasy truce. I even learned to see their scurrying as a reminder that the world went on in spite of my troubles. But, despite or because of success on the home front, I wasn't ready to go into town again. I couldn't check out any library books until I paid my fine, and even more, I was afraid I'd run into Diane and her biker boyfriend. Instead, on weekends I sat with Paul in the sauna. On Saturdays I would sit in the extra lounge chair and watch Paul as he circled the back yard, trying to smoke out the moles.

One early morning while walking home from work, a bald eagle soared above me, its white head and broad wings the rarest of promises in that area. I took it as a sign. I made a detour. It was almost six and the sun was about to come up. The sky had already turned from that solid dark to a gray haze that made you think you could see more than you really could. If I hadn't lived there or seen the beat-up Nova parked in front, I would have never been able to pick the small trailer out from all the others, each indistinguishable except for the lives that were in them.

She was slumped on the kitchen table, her eyes closed, her nose and mouth curtained by her brown hair. The fluorescent bulb in the ceiling struck a harsh light on her and the half-empty Wild Turkey on the table. A few embers glowed from the tin can stuffed with cigarettes that rested next to the bottle. The portable radio was on the edge of the table. I pressed my ear to the kitchen window. I recognized the DJ from the classic rock station we'd listen to well into the darkest time of night.

I wanted to walk in the door and turn off the radio, pick Diane up like a sleeping child and put her to bed, but instead I just watched her there, her face half-hidden with that thick hair I'd hidden my own face in so many times. Even through the glass I convinced myself that I could breathe in her scent of liquor and cigarettes and something sweet and unnamable that was integral to her skin.

I walked a window down to the boy's bedroom, which was more like a closet, just big enough to squeeze in a single bed and a beat-up dresser. He was illuminated by the reading light next to him, sleeping soundly, tangled in his sheets, hair matted to his face. Still afraid of the dark, I thought, even though Diane and I had both tried to rid him of that. But with all the changes, she'd probably given up that battle, at least for the time being.

That week at school we'd not said much to each other while we ate. There was too little and too much to broach at an elementary school cafeteria, so we reverted back to comfortable silence, the way we had done when I'd lived with him. That last day he asked me if I was coming back. I told him probably not.

"Thought so," he said, before downing the last of his milk straight from the carton. "Have a good life."

That killed me. A six-year old saying that kind of crap.

I finished my milk. We had matching milk moustaches. "You, too." Then, trying to make a lame joke I added, "Live long and prosper." I gave him the Vulcan sign, and he returned it, although I don't think he even knew what it meant. I wondered if this was all that would remain between us, the shared memory of that week of lunches together, a secret to everyone in the world except us.

It wasn't long after I had paid my visit to Diane and the boy that the truce between me and the rats ended. It was a Friday night, and I'd come off four nights in a row at the convenience store. I'd just made my nightly meal, a big bowl of popcorn drizzled with melted margarine and covered in salt. I had my radio hooked up to the classic rock station and was relaxing on the bed, grooving to some Deep Purple, the popcorn bowl secured between my thighs, when Paul huffed up the stairs. It was the first time he'd set foot in my bedroom since I'd moved in.

"I could use your help," he panted.

"After I finish my popcorn."

"It's kind of an emergency."

The back yard was on fire. Paul had gotten the idea that instead of mowing the lawn he'd burn it, a controlled burn kind of thing that had turned uncontrolled rather quickly. The flames were lapping toward the outhouse. We doused the fire with pails of water from the cistern, stemming it before it reached the outhouse boards. We beat the remains with the spare lunch trays, tramping the ash into the bare ground. When it was all over, Paul set his chair back on the ravaged lawn and took in the spectacle.

By the time I made it back upstairs "Smoke on the Water," was long over, and "A Whiter Shade of Pale," was playing. I'd read once that when the song came out the Beatles used to play it endlessly when they were tripping, and for some reason I hated the song after that. I sat down on the bed and laid the curtain over my legs like a tablecloth. The popcorn was no longer warm and the margarine had started to harden. I picked up a handful and shoved it in my mouth. After my first chew, the acidity told me something wasn't right, and I spit the mess onto the curtain. While I was helping Paul with the fire, the rats had taken over the room and pissed on my popcorn.

"Screw this!" I threw the bowl of popcorn onto the floor then stomped on the scattered kernels leaving them for the rats. Outside the sun was setting. I joined Paul on the loungers and watched the red and yellow sky recede to black, an artist's re-creation of the fire we'd just put out. Then Paul pulled out a few sheets of newspaper. He rolled one up and walked to a part of the yard that had not been burned. He lit the paper and stuffed it in the hole. After a few seconds, the smoke emerged from the other end.

"You think we could smoke out those god damn rats instead? They pissed on my popcorn."

Paul rubbed his cheek. "This requires some rumination. One mistake and the whole house could burn." He rolled a joint of weed grass and settled into his lounger.

"Well, ruminate, damn it, and make it quick."

"Some things take time," Paul said.

We waited for the moles to escape their smoke-filled tunnels, but none appeared. Finally, after the sun had set and it was dark, Paul stood and stretched his arms.

"Let's burn us some rats."

But for some reason I couldn't get up. The moment had passed, and like with Diane, I'd lost my will to fight. Paul didn't seem to notice. He was busy collecting things he could burn, trash, newspaper, twigs. Soon he had a respectable pile of combustibles under my bedroom window.

"No sense burning the house down," I called from my lounger. "I'll learn to live with them."

"Can't turn back now," he said. He lit the rolled up newspaper and watched the paper burn for a few glorious seconds before throwing it into pile. Paul whooped in delight. Twigs snapped under the flames.

I turned my attention to the moles, hiding in some secret recess of the home they had dug. The night surprised me with its sudden cold darkness. I picked up a piece of newspaper stacked next to where Paul had been sitting and rolled it tight. I lit it and stuck it one of the black dirt holes in front of me, then I stood up and started walking.

By the time I'd reached the bar, the stars were out in full force. I could see Denise and her biker boyfriend huddle at a table, sloppily holding each other up, their half-finished beers cigarettes momentarily forgotten. I thought about the boy and how he was sleeping right now in that little room of his, the lamp light burning beside him, and I kept walking.

When I arrived at the trailer park, the cold was no longer getting to me. It was an outside force that I'd mustered the strength to pretend wasn't there. Their door was unlocked, and I tried to be quiet, not wanting to scare the kid. The boy was just as I'd imagined him, sleeping under a tunnel of blankets, the light glowing. Leaning down, I woke him by rubbing his back the way I used to, hoping my hands weren't too cold. When he opened his eyes, he didn't seem at all surprised to see me.

"Can I sleep here, too?"

He said nothing, but scooted over to allow a sliver of the bed and a patch of blankets for me to bury in. When I heard his breathing become heavy with sleep, I turned off the light. Huddled under the covers, I counted fires. I counted stars. I counted rats. I counted trays. I counted moles and the holes in the yard they were hiding in. There were so many of them all, so much counting to do, and yet I still couldn't fall asleep.

Trouble With a Capital P

by Arnold Johanson

The pool hall beckoned with flickering
fluorescents and walls of neon selling sin:
Hamm's, Grain Belt, Pabst Blue Ribbon.
Jerry Lee and Elvis rocked the juke box
to syncopated pool ball clicks. Cigarette
smoke blended with beer and a hint of vomit
to impart a scent to shirt and skin
impervious to Listerine and Sen-Sen.

When she caught a whiff of where I'd been
Mom reminded me, each time, that I was
never to set foot again inside that place
where heathen men hang out to smoke and drink,
tell dirty jokes and do all kinds of awful things
with pool hall Jezebels, those *loose* women.
I wasn't sure exactly what *loose* meant.
I knew where I would have to go to learn,
but billiard parlor women, tight or loose,
have no time for pimply boys.

Two girls my age showed up one day.
The pool hall loosened Linda's mouth,
as well as the top buttons of her blouse.

Melanie had a body more mature than she was.
Cracking jokes about cues and balls, the girls
whipped me at rotation, then suggested I go
with them to an abandoned house nearby.
I went, praying that Melanie
was as loose as rumor had it.

Toad Lady and Bubbs

by Harold Huber

Toad Lady produced a muffled thump as she sat on the street bench. Her four coats cushioned the shock, but one of them catapulted a button and sent it rolling toward the curb. She sprang, as quickly as the heavy layers allowed, and snapped up the button before it reached the gutter. Seated again, Toad Lady rummaged through her many paper bags and found the remaining "C" of a petrified doughnut. She held the prize high, winked and whistled at it, launched a brief inspection for pests, then began the serious business of breakfast.

Chewing was no longer a casual matter for Toad Lady. Her teeth had diminished in number and now lent a picket fence effect to her broad smile. Having little concern for the "outer woman," she didn't fret about the open spaces, but steering a lower tooth to meet an occupied socket in the second tier, required steady concentration. While repacking her bag and licking the last fragments of pastry from her fingertips, she caught sight of a welcome image.

Angling down the sidewalk, his knees and shoes apparently at odds as to which direction would be best, was a man who seemed to be the victim of strong winds. He was swathed in a peeling oilcloth slicker, shod in flapping galoshes and capped by a brimless hunting hat. The flailing vision's name was Bubbs. In spite of the circumambulations of the course, he soon stood smile-to-smile with Toad Lady.

"Good morning, Eleanor," Bubbs sang out in a silvery voice that argued with the sight of him. "Nice day, huh?"

"My name's Toad Lady." She burped as she spoke.

"Well, I don't call you that. I call you Eleanor. That's what I name you."

Toad Lady moved a couple feet down the bench in a gesture of hospitality. "Park it, Bubbs." Bubbs parked it and lit quite a substantial remnant of a Chesterfield.

"How come you want me to call you Toad Lady?"

"Cause that's my name."

"I don't like it."

"That's my name."

Biting onto the cigarette in order to free his hands, Bubbs lowered the neck of his raincoat further down his shoulders. After a few other adjustments in preparation for a long sit, he removed the cigarette and sent a bottom-heavy smoke ring sailing west.

"Where'd you get that name, Eleanor... 'Toad Lady'?"

"That's what they call me."

"How come?"

"Don't know. Guess I look like a Toad."

Bubbs studied her hard. He couldn't make out "toad" anywhere. Maybe her hair. Some of its colors were shades of gray - others were browns, yellows and various other earth tones. Of course he could only see the fringes. The bulk of her head was encased in a limp camouflage helmet. He figured her hair added up to a kind of brown... or used to. He admitted brown was toady, but shouldn't there be warts? Two round moles and a birthmark shaped like Beulah Lake, but no warts.

"I think you look more like an Eleanor." While Bubbs continued to study her, Toad Lady gave her companion the once-over. They had rendezvoused at the bench daily for over a week, but she hadn't noticed his specifics before. If she had any reason to hate the man, she'd call him "Turkey Neck." That's how it looked, especially now with his coat thrown so far back. But she didn't hate Bubbs. She liked him. Even when they first bumped bags, she'd liked him - liked his pretty voice and wide-mouthed smile. They put her in mind of the yellow mongrel she'd befriended at the dumpster behind the IGA store. Now she catalogued some of his other details. Green eyes, pointy chin, skimpy whiskers, long thin hands, puny shoulders. Yup... she liked him just fine.

"Toad Lady sounds disrespectful to me, Eleanor."

"Uh-huh. Say, Bubbs, what do you think about all that pope stuff?" Her tongue traced an expert slalom in and out of the picket fence. A trailing, rather dainty burp signaled she was ready for his answer.

"Pope? What about him?"

"Oh, he's getting out of jail."

"The pope ain't in jail. They don't put popes in jail, Eleanor."

"It's Toad Lady! Sure he's in jail. I read it in the papers."

"Naw… you musta got it mixed up. He ain't been in jail."

"He has too been! I read all about it just yesterday. It said he agreed to pay his back taxes, and he's going back to his wife, and the Eye-talian cops are letting him out, and he promised not to evade anymore… and they believed him.

"You know what 'shminka marska' means, Eleanor?"

"And he has to pay a big fine too."

"Know what 'shminka marska' means?"

"I read the papers every single day, so I guess I oughta know what's up."

"Know what 'shminka marska' means, Eleanor?"

"Toad Lady! No… what's that - Chinese or something?"

"Oh no!" Bubbs laughed hard. His skinny hands slapped together. His eyes squeezed shut and his Adam's apple bounced up and down. He laughed until an overweight tear plowed a pink trail down his cheek, passed his nostril and dangled from his chin. When the spasms subsided, he rocked back and forth awhile then, adjusting his coat, he turned to his benchmate.

"Chinese! That's a good one, Eleanor!"

"His wife a nun?" Toad Lady asked, unwilling to relinquish popish matters.

"Shminka's a Polish word. I learned it from a genuine Polish man."

"My people never were Catholics, so how should I know. They didn't say much about his missus in the paper. You ever a Catholic, Bubbs?"

"Oh sure, a couple of times. I've been to every kind of church they got. I sort of collect them. You know, like a hobby. Priests and sisters can't get married, Eleanor."

"Well, they did! And anyways, he ain't a priest. He's a pope."

"He musta used to been a priest."

"What's he - your best friend or something?"

"All the popes used to be priests. It's a promotion."

"Is there more than one of them?"

"What?"

"Popes?"

"Well, at a time. They only let one in at a time. Then, after he's in, he's pope. They got it all worked out… you know, bylaws."

"Hey Bubbs, want a doughnut?"

Bubbs shook his head eagerly and fidgeted with his collar as he waited for Toad Lady to find paydirt in her bags full of bags. He noticed one of her hands was bigger than the other. Did that make her a toad? He also saw that her wrists were slender and moved gracefully as she probed the crackling sacks. One of her two watches had no face. The other was unusually large and had a bright orange plastic wristband.

"That a kid's watch?"

"I know I got two doughnuts left here...someplace. Hold on."

"Oh that's ok. You got kids, Eleanor?"

Toad Lady ignored the question and began methodically removing items from the largest bag and placing them in careful stacks on the bench. Bubbs nodded his head in approval - a fellow collector. She clearly specialized in pizza cardboards. A pillar of grease-patterned, corrugated discs wobbled as she energetically continued the search. Several tightly rolled newspapers soon flanked the pizza tower. She topped the pile with a pair of shag slippers, then switched to a second bag. "I know they're here, so don't get itchy," she mumbled. Bubbs immediately got an itch, but refrained from scratching it out of politeness.

A boy being led by two black Labradors lurched in their direction. The dogs, having caught the scent of pepperoni, were straining toward the bench. Toad Lady threw herself across the exposed treasures and pinned her terrified eyes on the approaching beasts. With all the command of tone his adolescent voice could muster, and with heel-planted body leverage, the boy finally succeeded in hauling the dogs out of range. Bubbs' assuring words and encouraging arm-pats eventually made Toad Lady relax. After a renewed burst of excavation, she brought forth two flattened, elliptical hoops of pastry.

"Hot dog!" Bubbs shouted— then, looking down the street, froze in mid-reach.

"What?" Toad Lady asked, as she turned to see what Bubbs saw. They were on their feet in an instant frantically stuffing the bench collection into its paper vaults. Things had apparently swollen because when the bags were packed, there was no room for the shag slippers. Toad Lady slapped her forehead. Bubbs grabbed the fuzzy objects and began wedging them into his slicker pockets. For a moment, a menacing finger aimed at him, but then withdrew when its owner remembered the emergency.

They soon stood side by side at the curb, trying to assume expressions of "waiting for a bus." A middle-aged policeman strolled up to them and smiled.

"Waiting for the bus, are you?" he asked Bubbs.

"Yup. Yessir. Thought I'd take in a little church today - seeing how it's Sunday and all."

"How about you, lady? I suppose you're going to church too."

"Oh yes I am, sir. I'm going to pray for the poor pope."

Uh-oh. Bubbs felt a panic feather brush the back of his neck. Eleanor mustn't start in on the jail story! She mustn't start sounding crazy... not to a cop. He scratched his neck and furtively shook his head in a "be careful" gesture to his friend. The officer looked up the empty street and asked what time they expected their bus. "Five minutes" and "Half hour" came out simultaneously. Then they both clammed up and waited for something drastic to happen.

Toad Lady, in her many-coated bulk, resembled a small monument. Beneath the final hemline, her legs were widespread and symmetrical. The two shopping bags hanging from each hand added to the balance of the design. Her helmeted head was bent low. Her tensed eyes peered straight ahead. Bubbs' anxiety took the form of perpetual motion. He shifted his weight rhythmically and kept looking up to the bus sign from different angles. He constantly jiggled the soda "pulls" in his pockets, kept there expressly to sound like the clink of coins.

"Say a little prayer for me when you get there. Say one for my feet," the officer added. "Get a decent job - you'll know what I mean."

"Oh it must be awful!" Toad Lady grieved at him, attempting to counterfeit a churchgoers concern for a fellow Christian.

"Yeah, this earning a living can be tough. Oh... that reminds me. I don't want to see either of you on this corner again. Understand?" Giving each of them a final, amused look, the officer walked away.

When they could no longer see the blue streak of him in the distance, the couple settled down again. Rearranging themselves on the bench with grinning, smacking lips, they returned to their morning meal.

"Where you sleeping tonight, Bubbs?"

"Downtown. How about you?"

"I'm behind the IGA now. It's pretty nice - got me a watchdog too. Here... want half of mine?"

"Sure! They're delicious, Eleanor. Know what 'shminka marska means?"

"What?"

"I learned it from a man right from Poland."

"What's it mean?'

"It means guinea pig. That's how they say 'guinea pig' in Poland.

Toad Lady looked away. She stared into space and remained silent, only blinking occasionally.

"Pretty good, huh, Eleanor? Isn't it funny how it sounds in Polish?"

No response from Toad Lady.

"I like the way it sounds. I wish I could talk Polish... don't you, Eleanor?"

Silence from his companion.

"I wonder how they say 'coffee' over there."

Neither spoke for a long time. Toad Lady's lids were closed. Bubbs finished the last of his doughnut and brushed an avalanche of crumbs to the sidewalk.

"Mine's name was Violet," she whispered into her hands.

"Yours what?'

"My guinea pig."

"Oh... shminka marska."

"I used to dress her up in dresses and have her play bride."

"Pardon me, Eleanor. I can't hear you."

"I made her her own house in my room. It was out of a Rinso case. She had a bed and a couch... with ruffles, but she liked it best to sleep with me."

"Uh-huh."

"She liked doughnuts too."

"Uh-huh."

"She never had any babies. Couldn't, I guess."

"Mine's name was Roland."

"Guinea pig?"

"Dog."

The Tree on the Curve

by Warren D. Woessner

Twenty years ago it folded a '57 Chevy
outside a bedroom where two folks
were glad to get up early, not thirty feet
from Roy Elroy's last fast ride.

That car became a lesson at the County Fair.
The posts and poles went right back up
along with a new sign like a snake.
The famous tree was propped up with cement.

Then the only cheap thrill was your ride.
Kids who missed Roy mixed in with his dash
played double or nothing on a dare,
and someone stole the cross.

Tires still burn at sixty, stupid bluff.
The ghost of Sharptown curve stands pat,
ready to raise the limit, rake in
all the chips again.

Zen Roses

by Alan Davis

He brought a plastic baggie to the Tupperware party, a baggie filled with golden globes of tofu fried in olive oil, flavored with basil and garlic and just a hint of pesto. It was his hot dish. He put two teaspoons of olive oil in the baggie with the tofu, which was extra firm, to keep it fresh, and rushed to his car, where in his haste he mashed his thumb in the door, but didn't let it slow him down on his way to the party as night draped over the city; a big one-eyed moon in the sky stared at him. At a stop sign, he could see a message fluctuating in neon, half-hidden by brick: zen Roses $9.95.

At the party, he brushed past Lucy, the hostess, with a quick kiss. "I have tofu," he said. "I want everyone - everyone - to have a taste."

"Great," she said. "I hope you left your attention span at the door. It's that kind of party."

The doorbell rang like crazy; Lucy had invited almost everyone—men, women, students, vagrants, circles of friends from her wayfaring who had never before been seen in the same place. She was a wreck, synapses and hormones firing too fast for her to translate, aflutter with detail and fuss. Any sensation but boredom had long been her motto, and she waved a hand like a magic wand in the direction of the Tupperware lady, who was dressed in polka dots and stood by the stove with painful good will etched on her pursed lips.

"Quick," he said, "I need a frying pan. I need to heat my tofu."

"Tofu?" the Tupperware lady said.

He found a frying pan and splattered some extra virgin olive oil inside it.

118

A few minutes later, he filled a borrowed Tupperware bowl with simmering tofu, firm spiced tofu that smelled of basil and garlic and pesto.

By then the place was packed, and everyone had been given a piece of Tupperware, a party favor at Lucy's expense. "The deal," she said, is two things. One, Tupperware. Buy something to help the cause. Two, speak in tongues, three minutes of talk. Speed talking. Talk for three minutes, then stop and listen. It's the way things are these days, with the war and all. You can say whatever the hell you want, but stop each time the buzzer sounds." It was like speed dating. The buzz of words filled every otherwise empty space, like a mind in overdrive. Not everyone had something to say, but those who didn't speak grimaced in embarrassment if the humor turned vulgar or nodded with a smile stuck to their faces or found a glass and poured a big drink.

The polka-dotted lady tried to interrupt but gave up and complained. "Is there anyone here with an attention span?"

"What?" he said, but then forgot what she wanted. He went around the room with his tofu and made certain to offer a taste to everyone.

Some stared at it in disgust or bewilderment.

"Yuck," one said. "Is that, like, you know, bean curd?"

"You eat that?" the polka-dotted lady said. "With what? Some kind of sauce?"

"It's great," he said. "Like monkey brain." He picked up a dripping globe between his fingers and held it to her nose. "It takes on the flavor of whatever you cook it in."

The look of disgust on her face made him think that she was hallucinating, and that what she saw in the bowl was a nest of squirming earthworms. "No," she said, flinching, and then forced herself to add, "thank you."

"You're welcome," he said. "It's not for everyone." He kept thinking of that sign: zen Roses. Only $9.95. It sounded wrong, putting a price on zen.

He had no attention span that night, it wasn't allowed, but, all appetite, he plunged into the tofu with zest. The polka-dotted lady flinched. She let out a gasp, as though the globe of flesh between his fingers was a sin that her priest had advised her against. She cocked her head and stared at him instead of the tofu. He could tell that she was transferring her disgust from the tofu to him. He could see that he had become the disgusting thing, like an earthworm in a bowl, but that didn't stop him, in fact it pleased him, he was appetite and desire and there was only one thing he wanted. "More tofu, everybody?" he shouted. He chewed each globe with delight, and to describe the taste would take more time than was available, an attention span longer than the one at hand that night.

"I could eat it all night," he said.

Lucy heard him. "Don't get cute about it, just help me pass stuff around and make sure everyone's happy." She studied the crowded apartment with eyes wide open in wonder, amazed that everybody she had invited had actually showed up, far too many people for her place to accommodate. "It's like performance art, isn't it?" She stared into his bowl and licked her lips, and he could see that she liked tofu, but half a dozen people at once screamed out her name urgently from across the room. Everybody wanted her attention, but by arrangement that night she had left it behind.

Hours later, worn out, people drifted into the dark world and the polka-dotted lady gathered her Tupperware, thanked Lucy, and made for the street, but he sat on the floor with his legs crossed and did not let the Tupperware lady have his plastic bowl - yes, it was his now - because good tofu was still in it. He intended to eat it all, every bit, and if someone wanted a piece, they could have it, he would share with everyone, pure frigging zen, but they had to ask, because if life has taught him one thing, it's that tofu is an acquired taste.

When he looked up from his bowl, almost empty now, the place was empty, except for Lucy, standing over him, catching her breath, and the six people who had all screamed so urgently for her attention. Her synapses were still firing off too fast, her attention span still in deficit.

"Just us," she said to the room.

Though it was late at night, she hadn't yet drawn the drapes, and the one-eyed moon still hung high in the sky, as though simmering in olive oil and basil. "Big olive oil moon," he said, pointing, and held out his clasped hands to her, as if holding a bouquet. "Zen roses."

She accepted the bouquet and stared out the window at the big baloney moon, as if seeing for the first time that it always promised way more than it could ever deliver. She broke open a bottle of lime-flavored gin and found a plastic baggie that contained a joint as thick as his swollen, throbbing thumb. "Enough with the moon," she said. She drew the drapes and sat cross-legged on the floor with a bedraggled sock monkey in her lap while they exhaled smoke rings. She pointed between his legs to the bowl. "Is there any tofu left?" When he shrugged, she said, "I tell you what. Let's you and me finish it off, right now. I mean, right now. I can't wait."

He offered her the bowl. She reached for it, like really fast, before their attention spans could come back.

The Last Black Eye

by Christine Holm

A number 4 pencil
Drew his dark things:
Hand-rubbed shadows in the hollow parts of breastbone, lip, and temple,
Bold and blurry question marks,
Rows of daggery dots across inverted exclamation points
So heavily graphited that they
Dully pewterized.

It was a fine tool for slashing, too:
Serrated the rumpled black-eyed page
(her jagged edges shorn from
Rips and tears, shreds turned wads
So tightly balled they could
Dry deadly hard this time).

But it was, finally, snapped into
The back of an institutionally pink room,
Where he took drawing lessons in a thin gown;
was the splintered part with no eraser and
The counter-sunk to bare-wood molar marks
That he put there, himself.

They calmly presented clean ragstock and a sharpened number 2;

Expected illuminations; promised me pastels.

There came years, then, of slow divergence from that old master
Some time hiding in hotels and in rental cars running under his nose,
Disappearing in broad daylight in between the stark lines of realism.
Later, there were court rooms lined with young lawyers
With their layers of metallic legalese burnished into records
That floated among offices in several states in an Escherized sort of way—
One hand shaking the other and attached to themselves at the source;
There was no true perspective in those pen-and-ink times.

Later, there were colleges and classrooms and professors of poetry,
And I took up with polymers and acrylics, indulged in Warhol strips of happy times,
Impressionistic streaks of cerise, some hours of celadon, a few blocks of Mondrian order.

But when the real oils came last year, and the muddy, sensuous earth of slip
Settled in the steady hot heat of his wood-fired kiln,
I came to know this new One slowly
Quietly, and greenly, like a tree budding in a hard spring
Through a season of waving grasses and autumn-leafed collages,
Then—it was then I transposed language and brush
Into this new abstract of blood and cells
And left the world of art behind.

Late Harvest

by Ellaraine Lockie

He meets them for coffee at the Q Cafe in the morning
Men who could have walked out of the Charlie Russell
print on the wall on their bowed legs
Rigged in Stetsons and scuffed cowboy boots
that hide bald heads and bunioned feet
Long-sleeved shirts with snaps and bled-out Levis
that cover long-johns even in 100-degrees

Their bull elk demeanors work hard
at making the coffee klatch look like coincidence
It wouldn't be manly to need camaraderie
Accomplices who agree about the new espresso shop
where shots are two bucks each
Some Goddamned California invention
Not like when coffee was
twenty-five cents with free refills

Men who lived the outhouse and cattle rustling story
in the *Way Back When* column of this week's *Mountaineer*
And drank boiled barley water together
through the depression

Moving into town close to the medical and senior

centers might have been the right thing he tells himself
But work ethics speak louder than shooting the bull
even if his son won't hear of it

So after an hour he climbs in his truck
and heads for the ranch
Carrying his rifle, an expired driver's license
And a can of oil to bribe the joints
of an old combine into one more season

Red Wisconsin

by G. L. O'Connor

We had nicknames for all the hoboes and farm workers who came to town each summer and fall. Usually we named them for the state they hailed from. Tall, lean and slick-haired "Tennessee" was from a small town just east of Nashville. And bow-legged, cowboy-booted "Tex" was a roving ranch hand from near Lubbock. "Husker" came from Nebraska, and "Okie" came from Oklahoma. Other years there were men from other states, and they were named accordingly. Most of these men were friendly and well-liked.

The fall of 1941 was different. That was the fall when Red Wisconsin came to town. He was scary and mean. We never knew what his real name was, but his nickname was "Red" and he came from Wisconsin, so we called him "Red Wisconsin." It made sense to us kids. We could have nicknamed him just "Wisconsin," or even just "Red," but we thought he might like either of those, and we had no intention of doing anything to please a bully like him.

Everybody knew about Red almost from the day he hit town. He had been sent by the Crystal Sugar Company to get the sugar beet receiving dump up and running, and to manage its operation through the beet harvest. He was short, stocky and strong. He had "weight-lifter" shoulders and arms, and could lift heavy things. He always seemed to be angry. And mean.

Red was a pusher and a shover. He would push his way through a crowd of people, and if anyone objected he would shove them. Most people in our town were nice mind-your-own-business folks so no one challenged him. He was nasty to folks in the cafe and grocery store.

Especially to kids and older people. Anyone who couldn't fight back. And when he drank he got meaner and his red face got redder. And he drank mostly on Saturday nights.

I remember Red even now, many years later, when harvest season comes around. The smells of barley dust and potato dirt take me back to that fall. The depression was nearly over, the war was about to begin, and financial relief was just around the corner. But, of course, nobody knew any of that yet.

I remember it as a time of poor roads, few cars and very little money. I was nine years old and had hardly ever been out of my Red River Valley home town of five hundred wonderful, durable farm people.

Winter was cold and not much fun. We didn't have hills to ski or slide on. Spring was nice, but it was wet and sloppy. The ground was thawing and gave off great smells. Summer was swimming in the city pond. Of course, we had lawns to mow and other jobs to do. But fall was my favorite.

Fall always had something special about it. More than any other season. Even the smells and colors were different. Grass was browning; the sunlight was a different color; people were burning leaves; other leaves lay on the ground smelling wet and moldy. There was an electricity about fall that no other time of year had.

It meant going back to school. Then Halloween. And then Thanksgiving. And before you knew it, Christmas when the two windows of Gundt's store would be lit with red and green lights and filled with toy displays. No other time of year had so much to offer a kid.

Even our folks felt it. The crops were "made." Now all they had to do was get them in the bin before the fall rains or early frost or late hail got them. It meant they could soon pay all the year's bills. And there were the church suppers.

When everything was done in the fields all three churches would each take their turn having their fall supper. We Catholics would have to borrow the Methodists' tables and the Lutherans' chairs, and they'd both borrow our silverware and salt and pepper shakers. Of course, everybody in town went to all three suppers. They were major social events. Fall was a lot of fun. Especially on Saturday nights. And that's where Red Wisconsin came into the picture.

The usual Saturday routine for us kids was to get our chores done early, take a bath if we if we couldn't get out of it, eat supper fast, get fifteen cents from Dad, if he had enough for all of us, then meet Rick, Ronnie, Toad, Louie and all the rest of the guys at the show hall for the movie. The

Gashouse Gang, the Dead End Kids, maybe even Abbott and Costello. We thought it couldn't get any better.

Ten cents got you into the movie. The nickel was for "whatever," afterward. Sometimes Dad gave us each a quarter. Then we really had a time after the movie. Coke and Pepsi were a nickel; candy bars were a nickel; ice cream cones were a nickel. Everything in the world cost a nickel. And when you had the nickels Saturday night was a great time.

The movie would start at seven-thirty and get out about nine-fifteen. Most of us didn't have to be home until ten-thirty on Saturday. It never took us long to spend our nickels so, with almost an hour until bed check, we'd look around for other sources of income. This was usually the drunk harvest workers in Stubb's tavern.

On Saturday evenings in the fall Stubb Backman's wife would set up a little two-burner gas stove just inside the tavern's open front door. She would grill hamburgers and onions for the hungry customers. It kept them from interrupting their drinking to go somewhere else for food. You could smell those buttery onions and the hamburgers half way down the block and made you want one so darn bad. But a hamburger cost fifteen cents. Everything we had.

Most of the harvesters started drinking before we went in to the movie, so by the time we got out of there and got our nickels spent they had about reached the "generous" stage. If we smiled and spoke to them politely they usually gave us a nickel or two. Not Red Wisconsin.

Red would usually swear at us and complain to Stubb about "Lettin' kids come into a place like this." Stubb would limp out from behind the bar on the wooden leg he earned in the Argonne Forest and usher us out. We liked the smell of Stubb's place — beer, cigar and cigarette smoke, Copenhagen snuff and open spittoons — so we hated to have to leave. We also liked to look at the big mirror on the south wall behind the bar. It was framed on each side by a silver naked lady holding a silver greyhound on a silver leash. We knew we weren't supposed to see it and that made it all the better.

Red Wisconsin was just one of many harvest gypsies. We had a lot of them. Nice guys like Joe Mallard, John Griff and my favorite, old Jim Durham. They came every fall, usually worked for the same farmers, were good to kids, polite to older people, and drank too much. There were some younger guys, too, but we didn't like them as much. They were in their twenties or so, wore tight T-shirts and big belt buckles. They liked to strut around and show off to the local girls.

One Saturday night I found old Jim sitting on the curb around the corner from the front door of Chick's Cafe. At first I didn't see him in the dark. He appeared to be drunk. His head was down and he'd been stomach-sick. Hoping for another nickel, I walked over and said, "Hi, Jim."

His head bobbed up, his speech was slurred. In his Texas drawl he said, "Boy, kin yuh he'p me to muh place?" Jim had rented a shed in the alley behind Chick's Cafe and Ocker Beck's Hartz Store. During the week he lived out at Horst's, the farmer who hired him each year, but he knew he would get drunk on weekends and he didn't want them to see him like that. Especially their kids. Jim liked kids. So he had a cot in this shed on weekends.

It was a double-sized "Roosevelt." That's what they called the wooden outdoor toilets that the WPA paid local men to build in the 1930's. There were one-holers and two-holers in back yards all over town. Jim's place was not a toilet. It was a solid bottom shed bigger than a four-holler, usually used for storage.

In the dark Jim eased himself down onto his cot and tried to say something to me. It smelled bad in there, as if someone had actually used it for a toilet. I thought his breath smelled sort of funny, too. Like vomit and beer and bubble-gum all mixed. He held me by the arm and wouldn't let go of me, at first. That scared me. Then he went to sleep or passed out sitting there, and I ran between the buildings out to the street where there was light.

Dad was standing in front of Chick's talking to another farmer. I was still a little scared so I told him about old Jim, and how he had held on to me and that he had smelled funny. Dad told me to stay there in front of the cafe, then he and the other man went into the Hartz store. Through the window I saw them talk to Mr. Beck who picked up a flashlight and all three of them went out the back door to Jim's shed.

It turned out that Jim had eaten some food that he'd left too long in an opened tin can. If Dad and the others hadn't taken him to the doctor right away he'd have died. Of course, Jim said that I was the one who had saved his life. After that he gave me dimes and quarters, and always told people, "That there red-headed, freckle-faced rascal saved ol' Jim's bacon. Yessirree." He said it so often that I began to believe I had.

Some farmers said that Jim was the best man they'd ever had on the place. Honest, reliable and strong. One said he was made of rawhide. Tough. That he knew how to pace him-self to outlast younger men. He was well past fifty, lean and sort of sad-looking when he wasn't smiling. A tall round-shouldered, slow moving man who usually went out of his way to avoid trouble. But Stubb Backman told Dad that when Jim finally got mad he got serious-looking, and could move pretty fast. Especially with his hands, which were surprisingly strong.

Once, when threatened by two younger men, Jim ripped two legs off one of Stubb's poker tables with his bare hands. Holding one leg in each hand like clubs, and without swinging even once, he just stood where he was and told the two men to pay for their drinks and leave. They did. Jim didn't raise his voice the whole time.

Red Wisconsin saw it. Everybody in the place saw it. When it was all over and people were back to talking and slapping Jim on the back, someone passed the hat around to get up some money so that Jim wouldn't have to pay for Stubb's broken table. That's how people felt about Jim Durham. When the hat came to Red he snarled, "Hell! Any yella belly that has t' use a club t' fight his fights can pay for his own damn table."

Jim just smiled and turned back to his friends, ignoring the liquored remark. Several others gave Red hard looks, but looked away quickly when Red scowled at them. That's how people felt about Red Wisconsin.

❦   ❦   ❦

On a Saturday night in early October, after the movie, Ronnie Dahl and I went into Stubb's place to try our luck on the drinking workmen. Grain harvest was over and many of the older men had moved back south for the winter. Potato and beet harvest was colder, harder work and the bones and bodies of most of the older men were no longer up to it. Now the rowdier, younger men were in demand.

Jim Durham was one of the few older harvesters still in town. He was at a table near the booths on the north side of Stub's barroom playing cards with three other men. He smiled at me when we came in and I headed straight for his table. One of his companions smiled and greeted me with, "Hi there, Little Red." Jim slipped a quarter into my hand.

Red Wisconsin was at the next table, his face red from drinking. He turned and growled in our direction, "Who you callin' 'Red'? That's MY name." He reached for my arm.

Jim pulled me out of Red's reach, laid his cards onto the table and in a soft voice said, "You don't touch this here boy, Red."

The laughing and talking stopped. Everyone turned to watch. I was scared. Ronnie ran outside. I'd have run, too, but Jim was still holding my arm. Stubb came around from back of the bar hoping to head off a fight by scolding me, "I told you kids to stay..."

Red cut him off. "MY name's 'Red'!" He glared at me, "Don't you ever let me hear you callin' yerself 'Red'."

Jim still had his hand on my shoulder. It dug into me just a little when he told Red once more, "You don't touch this here boy." Both men were still sitting.

Stubb got between them, took me by the arm and headed me toward the door, making sure that Red couldn't reach me as we went. "I don't want you kids in here on a Sattidy night. It's no place for you. Now, twenty-three skiddoo," and he guided me out the door.

Ronnie was waiting for me around the corner of the tavern. We looked in through a place in the window where the Schmidt Beer sticker had peeled back. Red and Jim were still sitting at their tables. They weren't looking at each other and they weren't talking at all. The other men started to talk and move around again, but Jim and Red just sat there. Jim looked serious again.

It was almost ten-thirty so Ronnie and I lit out for home after one more peek at the silver naked ladies back of the bar. As we crossed the railroad tracks by the Peavey elevator I said, "If Red had tried anything Jim woulda clobbered him, I bet."

Ronnie sort of agreed. "Yeah . . . Jim's pretty old, though. But I bet some of the other guys woulda helped."

"Jim wouldn'a needed any help. He's strong!" I bragged without conviction.

The block and a half from the elevator to Ronnie's house was open pasture and had no street lights. We ran the distance without a word, all the time imagining we could hear someone, probably Red Wisconsin, in the tall grass alongside the path. Couldn't have been just crickets.

We didn't waste any time on "Good Nights." Ronnie ran in the house. I was half out of breath so I walked to the corner of Ronnie's yard and puffed 'til I caught my breath. From Ronnie's house to my house on the edge of town there were several street lights, but I was all alone so I ran the entire two and a half blocks wide open.

In our town either you were a farmer or you worked for one. Unless you owned a store or gas station or something. We were farmers. Our house was on the southeast corner of town. Go out the front door and you were in town. Out the back door you were in the country.

Dad and Mother were having coffee in the kitchen when I came in the back door puffing. I told them about Red and Jim. Mother didn't like it. "You should not have been in Stubb's." Dad looked angry, but didn't say anything.

The kitchen was right below my bedroom. After I went to bed I could hear them talking, but couldn't catch quite what they were saying. I heard Dad's voice. He mentioned Red's name and, ". . . do something about. . ." Then I heard the screen door open and close, heard Dad get in the car and drive off toward Main Street. I remembered that he hadn't said anything while I was in the kitchen, but he looked very serious. Dad had been our county sheriff and was a state trooper before resigning to take over the family farm. My dad could handle anything.

❁   ❁   ❁

That Wednesday it rained. It was the slow kind of drizzle that lasts all day. The beet and potato crews shut down, drew some pay, put on clean T-shirts and headed for town. It was like Saturday in the middle of the week, except that we kids had school until four o'clock and a nine o'clock curfew on school nights.

After supper five of us kids were playing "keep-away" with a soft ball in the soggy lot between the cafe and the Hartz store, and making a lot of noise when Rick Keely said, in a sort of a loud whisper, "There's Red!" When I turned to look he was right beside me. His face was redder than usual and he looked mean. He smelled bad, too. Like beet dirt and dirty clothes. He grabbed my arm.

Ronnie yelled, "Look out! He's got a knife!"

Red had a big black-handled jackknife in his right hand, with the long blade opened. He let go of my arm and grabbed me by the ear so fast that I didn't have a chance to run. He grinned, "Awright, 'Little Red.' Should I cut off one o' your ears? Or maybe that red hair o' yours?"

He laid the edge of the knife blade against the back side of my ear. Ronnie told me later it was actually the dull side of the blade, but I couldn't tell. I was scared. My ear hurt me the way Red was pulling on it, but the guys were all watching so I couldn't cry.

Then I heard Jim's voice. He wasn't loud or excited. He spoke almost softly. "Red. I told yuh not t' touch this boy." He must have heard Ronnie when he yelled about the knife. His shed was right behind the Hartz store.

Red hadn't moved so Jim spoke again. "I said you don't touch this here boy, Red. I told yuh." Red let go of my ear and faced Jim, the knife still in his hand. Now that I was able to run away I didn't know if I should. I just stood there watching both of them.

"He's a smart-aleck kid," Red said. "I was just takin' him down a peg or two. He went cryin' to his ol' man about last Saturday night, an' his ol' man came shootin' off his mouth to me. If you ask me, the whole damn family needs takin' down a bit. Might just do it, too."

Still speaking quietly Jim said, "Red, I'm gonna buy you a drink. We got some talkin t' do. I'll join yuh in Stubb's direc'ly."

Red surprised us. He didn't say anything. After a moment he folded his jackknife, turned and headed for Stubb's front door, but not without a mean glare at me. "Be seein' you around."

Jim put his hand on my shoulder, smiled, gave me another quarter. "You boys get your-se'fs some sody-pops." To me he added, "And don't you worry. Red ain't gonna bother you no more." Then he went into Stubb's tavern, too.

Inside Chick's Cafe Ronnie, Rick, Toad and Louie and I each had a bottle of pop on Jim's quarter and talk-bragged about what had just happened. From behind the soda fountain part of the counter Chick said he didn't believe us. Neither did Trygve Bellman, the town cop. Trygve probably couldn't have done much about it anyway. He spent part of most evenings just looking out of Chick's front window trying to appear official. If any real trouble did arise he would call other citizens to help. It was nearing nine o'clock, and well past dark, so when he told us to finish our pop and high-tail it for home we did.

Toad and Louie headed for the north end of town where they lived. Ronnie, Rick and I lived on the south end. We walked slow looking in as we passed Stubb's. Jim and Red were at a table talking. Jim looked grim and old. Red looked angry and scowly. I heard later that Jim bought Red three or four drinks, then left. Red stayed and drank some more. Of course, I told Mother and Dad about it when I got home.

This time Dad got really angry. "Damn!" He looked at Mother for a minute. "I think I'll drive downtown. Maybe have another talk with Red."

❦   ❦   ❦

The next morning school was called off. Parents were told to keep their kids home. That there was a killer loose in the area. Mr. McClannon, the Peavey elevator man, and Mr. Dailey, the depot agent, had found a body when they were inspecting grain cars. Trygve kept everyone away from the boxcar until the sheriff could come from the county seat twenty-four miles away.

It was Red Wisconsin, all right. With his black-handled jackknife stuck in his chest. "Just a little to the left of center," Trygve said. The sheriff deputized Dad and a few other men from town, and they searched the area and questioned lots of people.

Dad talked to Jim. Jim told him about what Red had done to me the evening before, and what he had said about our family. Jim said, "Nice family like yours oughtn't have t' worry about the likes of ol' Red, there. Well, I guess he won't bother nobody no more."

When the sheriff asked Dad about Jim, Dad hesitated a moment, then said, "Couldn't have been old Jim. He's too old and too light weight to handle a man of Red's heft." The sheriff agreed, and the two of them convinced the coroner of the facts in the case: that Red had been seen in a local tavern drinking heavily the night before; that he had evidently crawled into the open boxcar to sleep it off, a common practice; in the dark he had likely tried to stand up and had rolled or fallen on his own knife. Case closed.

Jim Durham returned to our town for five more harvest seasons. He always declined Dad and Mother's invitations to Sunday dinner, but would buy Dad a drink and would accept one in return to show that he appreciated the offer. He didn't come north in the spring of 1947. We learned that he had died in March, somewhere in Texas. I don't even know the name of the town.

The smells the potato dirt and barley dust in the fall always make me think of church suppers, Saturday night movies, Abbot and Costello and old Jim Durham. And Red Wisconsin, too.

Fireflies

by Jessica Del Balzo

You were drunk again and replacing light bulbs
in the middle of the night as Mick Jagger sang
about the Midnight Rambler. It wasn't that
you missed the old life, exactly, it was just that
this new way of shedding light on dark rooms was so much
quieter, so much so that you couldn't be without sound.

You were always saying that
you didn't understand
how I could be still without music or television or even
humming.

Most would have said your eyes needed screen doors
to keep the bugs out and the animals in, but I would have let you
take the hinges off
if that would have made you happy. I would have done
almost anything for you, but I promise you this:
I never would have tried
to be your lampshade.

I remember a night years before the old life had even
started, back before the city, back by the river
where fireflies lit the branches of the trees

framing us. The way you breathed
in that beautiful tainted sky, like it was the one thing
you knew no one could take from you, it made me want
to catch falling stars in my mouth and
hand them over.

Our little secret. They wouldn't
take away what they didn't know was there, kept tucked, pressed
against the roof of your mouth. I could trust you. Why couldn't you
trust yourself?

I would have kept them all
away, put up fences on the outskirts of your nightmares. I would have
picked your apples for you, cleaned them well, even let you run
your fingers over the soft parts of the bad ones
before burying them in the dirt.

But I think you liked the frantic
gathering, the heaviness against your thin arms. I think you liked seeing
how far you could walk without dropping
everything.

But baby, we're going to be old one day,
even you. And it's going to take a long time. So take
a rest. You're going to want to be ready for what
I wish you'd believe is still
yet to happen. Trust me. This is
what you won't want to miss, not that
cut-up darkness you carry in your eyes the way you used to
carry stars, the way the trees held fireflies.

I know
your arms are strong, I know you know how to run
between raindrops, how to pick up and
leave in the middle of the night, gritting
words between your teeth like pills.

But you can spit them out, and you don't need to
keep running. You don't need to replace any more
light bulbs either.

If you have to do something, start
opening windows. Morning is coming, and
I've got plans for me and you
to watch the sunrise. I'm telling you, I know
just the place, and it's right where you are.

Cold Hard Glare

by David Tookey

After the death of my friend
I was pissed and looking for
Some answers. Of course I
Tried counseling, therapy and
Read a variety of self-help books.
(How can you be expected to help
yourself at a time like this?)

So I wandered into a church one day
-Didn't matter what denomination-
Sat down in a pew, and took a good
Long look at the guy nailed to the cross.
I looked at him hanging there
and fixed him in my cold hard glare.

The church was still and I didn't
Really feel any answers to my grief
Or pain coming on. But, this was the first
Time in quite a while that I had
Experienced peace and quiet,
Just simple peace and quiet.

It occurred to me that maybe that was

What this place had to offer.
Maybe the answer to all the pain
And anger is just peace and quiet.
No explanations as to why
My friend was gone, no reasons, no excuses.

After a while I got up and left. None of my
Demanding questions had been answered; maybe that's the
Answer. These questions are unanswerable, so let them go.
You ask questions because you think answers to those
Questions will give you peace. Maybe by just stopping the
Asking we come closer to the peace we seek.

PART FOUR

The Memory of Water

by Mark Vinz

Here where the Sheyenne joins the Red—
upstream, the Bois de Sioux, and down,
the Buffalo—imagination finds its way,
like swirls of white stirred by the prairie winds.

These are the places towns were built,
water flowing underneath snow-covered ice
laced with the tracks of skis and snowmobiles
and creatures rarely glimpsed by passersby.

Today I'm home from the desert, where
two weeks of rain had finally broken—
arroyos carried everything away
except for the pools on asphalt roads.

How inevitably it all flows off and disappears—
water and what it has been named for—
here, in this glacial lakebed where I live,
still dreaming of the great herds passing.

The Oceanic Twins

by Jessica Del Balzo

You were sitting in a dark room near the beach with your fingernails glowing a salty shade of blue, and you were laughing. I asked you what was so funny, and all you said was something about room temperature and waking up.

"Feels like brick-laying," you said, and when I stepped to you I could see the salt on your cheeks.

Any other hour, and you would have been pounding away at your teal-colored typewriter, as you became prone to doing after I left, the beaded bracelets around your wrists touching against each other, calm, comforting, something tangible to keep you on dry land in the night.

I wanted to ask if you'd ever gone looking for me, grassy thoughts about fate and constellations in your head, through the streets, along the docks. There were nights that I would have sought you out, had I not already known where you were.

Did you ever look for my voice behind the gazes of men who were the kind of thin that kept you always on edges with them? Only now did it occur to me to be sorry I had never been there, if you even wanted me to be. It was hard to tell, the way all of a sudden you were looking so alive like this. I don't know what I'd been expecting, but certainly not to see the wallflower haze gone from your eyes.

"I think I missed you," I said, and you opened your palm to show me the compass tattoo with its silver needle pierced into the skin, spinning. That was when I knew I had come to the right place.

To Die For

by Joan Jarvis Ellison

At 5:17 a.m., the first few bars of *Golddigger* by Kanye West ripped Josh Brooks out a deep, satisfying sleep. He groped across the bedside table and grabbed his cell phone. "Wha?"

"Josh, Josh, I need you." He barely recognized the voice of his childhood best friend through the static.

"Pete? It's 5 o'clock in the damn morning. What's wrong?"

"You gotta come now. There's a red eye, at 5:30, your time, I looked on Orbitz. I'm gonna lose the resort. A man died. You gotta come help me out."

"Wait," Josh soothed. "Let me call you back. This connection sucks. Okay," he said, moments later. "You sounded like you were in the lake. You've got really crappy reception out there. I thought you said a man died."

"I did. James Broad. And I think they're gonna close the resort and arrest Mac for murder. Or me. You gotta come, Josh, please."

It was the please that caused Josh's brain to finally click on. Pete didn't beg, ever. "Start at the beginning. What happened to who, and especially when? It's 5 o'clock for God's sake."

"It's James Broad," Pete's voice quavered, "the restaurant critic, you know?" He paused for Josh's mumbled assent. "He was staying here. And he died. And after the ambulance came, the police came. And they said they thought he was poisoned and if it was food poisoning, they'll shut down the grill. And even if it wasn't food poisoning. Who would come stay at a resort where someone died. I'll lose the resort." Pete's words ran down into quiet.

Josh dragged his hand down his face, trying to pull some sense of alertness from his brain. "In the morning. I can call you in the morning and we'll figure this all out."

"There's another plane if you can't get the early flight. I checked on Orbitz. You can catch the plane at 5 p.m., that's the first flight out with room on it, get to Fargo by 8 our time and here by 9 or 10. Please Josh. I can't do this with out you."

"What do you expect me to do? I don't know anything about death."

"You're in advertising, with a corner office. You can figure out how to spin this so that we can stay open."

"Okay, okay. I'll bring Genevieve if I can wake her up in time to get packed." In all their years of friendship, Pete had never asked him for anything beyond a beer or a ride into town. This was one request he had to honor.

"I'll leave the lights on in your old cabin, number six. Thanks."

Josh dropped the phone and turned to the woman who lay snuggled against his thigh. He slid down beside her under the duvet and nuzzled the auburn curls that clustered around her head. "Genevieve?" Josh murmured. "Pack your bags, we're going to spend the weekend on the most beautiful lake in Minnesota."

Genevieve stretched and yawned. She looked up at him, eyelids still heavy with sleep. "What should I pack and when are we leaving?"

"It's a little resort," Josh said, rolling out of bed. "Dress casual. But we're leaving right after work today, so pack fast."

The rental car agency at the airport closed immediately after Josh and Genevieve picked up their car. Twenty miles out of Moorhead, Genevieve looked around carefully. "Where are the lights?" she asked.

"What lights?"

"Any lights. Street lights, house lights, car lights, any lights." Her face, in the dashboard lights, seemed strained.

"We're in the country, honey. No lights but ours. This is normal."

"This is not normal in any world I've ever heard of."

"You saw the movie "Fargo" didn't you," Josh glanced at her, his lips quirked.

Genevieve shuddered. "It's a good thing it's not snowing, or I'd hijack this car and head straight back to New York."

They turned off the freeway onto a two lane road. "I can't believe you grew up out here," Genevieve said to Josh. "It explains a lot about you."

"Like what?" He grinned at her. "My manly charm?"

"No, I was thinking more about your independence."

"And you, my lovely New Yorker, where did you get your independence? Damn!" Josh said suddenly, twisting the steering wheel into a swerve.

"What? What's that smell?" Genevieve gasped.

Josh sighed. "Skunk."

"I've never seen a skunk, and if they all smell like that, I don't want to. Speed up and get us away from the smell."

"Well, I didn't see that one either; I hit it. That smell will be with us."

They drove on through the night, past field after field rolling into the distance, lit only by moonlight. Then the road began to twist and soon they were running through a tunnel of trees, lit only by the headlights. "Look," Josh said. "See the two little green lights at the edge of the road? Deer eyes. What do you bet she's got a fawn or two with her." The doe loped across the road as Josh slowed the car to a stop. Then two smaller animals, their spots just fading, followed her.

"Wow," Genevieve said. "That was maybe worth driving where there are no lights."

Josh pulled the car into a driveway and stopped in front of a tiny house, lights glowing behind yellow and pink plaid curtains. "Welcome to Maple Beach Resort," he said, ushering Genevieve through the door.

"What is this place?" she asked sharply.

Josh glanced around at his childhood second home. The cream paint on the iron double bed frame was still flaking gently from around the rose flower decal. He recognized the curtains at the windows and the faded painting of a woodland garden on the wall. A yellow flowered quilt lay on the bed.

"What is this?" Genevieve repeated, looking at the small rose decaled dresser and the curtains hung in front of the clothes rod, at the tiny bathroom sink squeezed in next to the water heater. "The Bates Motel comes to mind"

Josh stared at her, some how surprised that she didn't share his childhood memories. "It's a local landmark, not fancy, but the sheets are soft, the quilts are warm, the food is great, and the owners are the best people in the world."

"Hey," said a voice from the doorway. Pete Nelson was standing there, grinning crookedly at them. He was struck by the sensuous beauty of the woman Josh had brought with him, and by her abrupt dismissal of the best cabin on the place. Bates Motel indeed! "Watch what you say about my home, Jennifer."

Josh winced. "Hey Pete, this is Genevieve." The two nodded cautiously at each other. Josh thumped him on the back. " Good to see you. Sorry it took a death to get me back here. Have a seat and tell us what's going on." Josh lounged on the bed, pulling Genevieve down next to him. Pete sat down at the small yellow painted table, pulled a daisy out of an old pink ceramic vase and began twisting the stem round and round his finger.

"This has been an amazing week," Pete said. "Jill has been down taking care of her mother, who's dying, off and on all summer. I've been parenting full time, and Jay has fallen in love with a rich muscle man with a cigarette boat. A cigarette boat! Why would anyone bring one of those here?"

Josh laughed and glanced at Genevieve. "A cigarette boat goes about a hundred miles an hour, zero to one hundred in sixty seconds and costs about a hundred thousand dollars. I think they're famous because James Bond drove one. Jay is Pete and Jill's daughter. She's six, so I don't think the love angle is too important." He turned back to Pete. "And you lust after the boat?"

"No way," Pete grinned. "It's out of my ball park. It does guzzle gas, so I'm making some good money off it. But having James Broad die in one of my cabins just takes the cake." He ran his hands through thinning sand-colored hair.

"Wait, wait." Josh asked. "I've seen a picture of that guy somewhere. He was immense. Why don't they think he died of a heart attack?"

"They did an autopsy, and he was poisoned! Here. Nobody will ever come again. We'll have to close."

"So I still don't understand; why you?"

"He'd been here for three weeks. He never went anywhere. He'd waddle out of his cabin about 11 o'clock, eat lunch, waddle back to his cabin, waddle out for supper, waddle back and we wouldn't see him again until the next day. At lunch time."

"Why did he come here?" Genevieve asked, disbelief obvious in her face and voice. "He was a celebrity food critic. If he didn't swim, sunbathe, or fish, didn't ride around in boats, why did he come here? Did friends visit him?"

Well, Guinevere," Pete said, "other than snoring, I never heard any sounds from his cabin. " He paused. "Actually, that's not right. I did hear him talking to some one about a week ago, but I never saw anyone." Pete shrugged. "But to answer your question, he came for the food. Said our grill was his favorite place to eat."

Pete saw the ripple of distaste cross Genevieve's face. Josh saw it too.

"Just wait for lunch, honey," he said, touching her shoulder. "Well, it's late for us and you look dead, Pete. I'll bring in our bags and in the morning we'll figure out what to do next.

Josh turned out the lights and slid beneath the quilt, cradling Genevieve's body next to his. From a distance, the voice of a loon floated eerily across the lake. Genevieve stiffened. "What was that?" she whispered.

Josh chuckled, "Relax, it's just a loon. As in bird, not as in insane. They were just drifting off to sleep when a sharp yipping filled the night air. "Coyote," Josh said when Genevieve shuddered. "Probably has pups in a den near here. Maybe we can find them tomorrow."

"If I haven't left by then," she muttered. "I am not impressed with your Minnesota. I expect wild Indians to ride out of the woods or a mad killer lurking behind the wood shed." She hitched herself up on one elbow. "Where is the wood shed?"

Josh grinned up at her. "I'll show you in the morning if we make it through the night."

Twisting poplar leaves dappled the sunlight streaming through the door when Josh woke. He stretched and smiled. Time to go fishing. Just like he had every other morning he'd wakened in this cabin. He slid out of bed, pulled on jeans and stepped quietly out the door. The cabin next door was barricaded with yellow police tape. Across the street, Pete was sitting on the steps down to the dock, staring out at the lake. The island still floated green and mysterious in the middle of all that blue. Reeds skirted the shore to the left and to the right, a red winged blackbird sang from its perch on a cattail stalk. A pair of mallards landed just beyond the end of the dock. Josh settled beside Pete and watched the waves lapping against the dock pilings, content in the quiet, sliding back into their old relationship. "How's fishing?"

"Sunnies and crappies are good. Northerns are getting smaller each year."

"Are your cabins full?" Josh asked. "I was surprised to get our old cabin."

"Anybody with young kids left immediately. The rest are more interested in

watching the police procedures than in running. I guess that's good. But Mac's going crazy with nothing to do."

"My God, where will we eat?" Josh grinned.

"I suggest the new coffee shop in town. They've ruined me for my own coffee. Or for a different menu, there's always the Rush-In."

"Same owners?" Josh asked.

"Same food." A grin flashed across Pete's face and then disappeared.

"Josh, I don't know what to do next. The police haven't closed the cabins, but I'm afraid they will if they can't figure out what happened. They've taken every body's name and address and asked about our whereabouts. The grill is closed until further notice and I have no idea when that will be. Mac's insulted that Brandon, you remember Brandon Johnson, he's a County Sheriff now, would suspect him. He's threatened to leave. And Jay's acting crazy, She has practically disappeared, hides out all day and only comes home after supper. I just don't know what to do."

" What do the police think?" Josh asked. "Who found him?"

"I did," Pete said grimly. "When he didn't come for lunch, and then didn't come out for dinner, I went into his cabin. He was just lying there, mouth open, big belly a mound under the quilt, and a fly hovering over his mouth. His face was pale, not his normal red. And he smelled bad." Pete swallowed. "I called 911."

I've got a spin idea," Josh said. "But it depends on the cabins and the grill being open into the fall. Sounds like that depends on figuring out who killed James Broad." He chuckled. "Where's John Grisham when you need him?"

"Yeah right, like any of us knows John Grisham."

"Genevieve does." Josh said. "He's one of her agency's authors."

A cabin door banged. "Josh?" Genevieve's voice.

"Down by the lake, Honey." Josh waved his arm.

Genevieve stepped onto the lawn and the heels of her white beach sandals sank into the sod. "Damn!" She danced backward trying to move and protect her sandals. "Josh, get up here and help me. This place has a mud-pit for a front yard. My heels are sunk."

Pete snorted. "Figures," he said under his breath. Josh started to his feet, grinning, but Genevieve had already wrenched her heels free of the goop and was striding down the driveway. "Follow the road, Ginger," Pete shouted. "We've had a lot of rain lately."

She was cursing as she stepped down onto the dock. "Listen, my name is Genevieve, get it straight! And where do I get some coffee?"

"Looks like we'll have to go into town," Josh said. How are your shoes?"

"Filthy," Genevieve said and tried to lift her foot. The narrow heel of her sandal was wedged between two dock boards. "Dammit!" she muttered, and slid her foot out of the shoe. She took a step, caught the second heel, and toppled into the lake.

Josh jumped to his feet. When Genevieve surfaced, Pete was laughing and Josh was trying not to. She grabbed a dock post. Her curls were plastered to her face, mascara ran down her cheeks, and her sleek white sun dress was streaked with green algae. As she pulled herself up onto the dock, a stringer full of fish slithered against her leg. "What!" Genevieve shrieked. "What is that?"

Josh pulled the stringer out of the water. "Nice sunnies," he commented. "That big one's a beauty."

Tears of laughter running down his face, Pete gasped for breath. "Those must be Jay's. She fishes every morning. She always cleans what she catches right away, I wonder why she hasn't cleaned them." He bowed slightly to the drenched woman. "Thanks, Jen," he said. "I really needed that laugh."

"My name is Genevieve," she snarled, and stalked back toward the cabin, leaving her heels on the dock.

"What do you see in her?" Pete asked Josh, suddenly sober.

"In New York, she seemed like a good idea," Josh said, "Beautiful, smart, funny. But she really hasn't adapted very well to rural life yet." He wrenched her heels out from between the dock boards. "I'd better go help repair the damage."

Genevieve was still simmering when they drove into town an hour later. She was dressed in black shorts and a bright green shirt with black sequined flip-flops on her feet. "You told me casual!" she said into a long silence.

"In what world are four inch heels at a resort casual?" Josh asked, surprised.

"My world." Genevieve lapsed back into silence.

"Give it a chance," Josh said. "You'll love it here."

"Yeah right," she muttered.

They rounded a bend in the road. "What are those huge things in that field? She asked.

Josh laughed. "They're old threshing machines, for separating the wheat seed from the rest of the plant. I used to pretend they were robot killing machines."

"Nothing would surprise me," Genevieve murmured.

❦   ❦   ❦

The coffee shop sign read "Closed on Sundays." Great, Josh thought. That leaves the Rush In. "Well, you're in for a real down home taste experience," he said to Genevieve as they parked in the single spot left on the street.

"It must be a good restaurant," Genevieve said. "It's packed."

Josh looked at the Sunday morning crowd of families in church clothes and shook his head. "Think of this as small town America." A waitress seated them at the last open table. "Two coffees," he told her. "And I'm having a beef commercial, real comfort food."

The girl handed a menu to Genevieve. "What kind of greens do you use in your salads?" Genevieve asked.

"Greens?" the girl asked. "What do you mean 'greens?'"

"Spinach, arugula, beet greens, cilantro, oak leaf lettuce, the possibilities are

endless."

"Lettuce." The waitress focused on the one word she recognized. "We use lettuce," She held out her hands as if clasping a ball, "you know, lettuce."

Genevieve groaned. "Do you put any vegetables in your salads? You know, vegetables, like tomatoes, peppers, beets?"

The girl flinched at her tone. "We have tomatoes and dill pickles on the salads."

Josh brushed Genevieve's knee. "Try a grilled cheese sandwich."

She sighed. "Okay, I'll have a grilled cheese on caraway rye with an extra slice of cheese." She looked at the waitress who was shaking her head. "What, no extra cheese?"

"White bread or wheat?"

"Wheat, please," Genevieve said.

"Do you want a pickle with that, Ma'am?"

Genevieve turned to Josh after the waitress had stalked away. "Did she just call me Ma'am? Do I look that old?"

"It's usually a term of respect around here. But this time, I suspect it was getting pretty close to a curse."

Genevieve simmered until the waitress laid a plate in front of her. "Grilled cheese on wheat with extra cheese, a pickle and chips. They come with it."

"Gee thanks." Genevieve turned to Josh. "How can this place survive?"

"You're in the country. This is good hearty food for farmers." He lifted a fork of potatoes and gravy to his mouth and smiled. "Too bad you're a vegetarian."

"Hey!" Josh jumped to his feet. "Mark. How the hell are you?" He gestured to the massive man walking into the restaurant. "Can he join us? He was one of my best friends. Great guy."

Josh introduced the two and then went off to find the waitress.

"So," Genevieve said, admiring the man's heavily muscled arms and shoulders. "Do you work out?"

"Nah," Mark said, "I just farm, but my wife works at the library."

Genevieve stared at him, utterly and completely lost. She picked up her sandwich and began to eat.

"So what are you doing in town?" Mark asked as Josh slid back into his seat. "Haven't seen you in a long time."

"Pete called. He's real worried."

"Well, he should be. Gossips going around like crazy. Some people say Mac's finally gone off his rocker. Others say Pete's housekeeping did the guy in. I think it's just bad luck, but Pete can't afford to lose many customers. None of the resorts around here are doing very well. They can make a lot more money for less work by selling their land as individual lake lots."

Josh choked on his sandwich. "Is Pete close to selling?"

Mark shook his head. "I don't know. He loves that place. I can't imagine him doing anything else. But without money, what's he gonna do?"

"Are locals staying away?" Josh asked.

"The grill is a big part of his income," Mark said.

"Okay. I guess we'll just have to design a campaign." Josh glanced at Genevieve's plate. "Hurry up, Love. We've got to get back to the cabin."

Josh checked Genevieve's closed expression several times on the drive back to the lake. Her eyes studied the greens and browns of the passing sloughs and the pasturing horses, intently. "Are you doing okay?" he finally asked.

She shook her head. "I feel like Dorothy. This isn't Kansas, Toto. I got off the plane and I haven't been myself since. I don't know how to dress, how to walk, how to order a meal. I can't even understand the language."

Josh laughed. "Now you know how I felt when I first came to New York."

"No," Genevieve argued. "You had college to prepare you. This is like nothing I've ever experienced in my entire life." She watched as the lake came into view behind the thin veil of golden leaves. "Don't leave me alone until I get acclimated."

Josh chuckled. "When we get back to the cabin, we'll go for a swim, maybe take a boat out, hope for the grill to be open for supper, and then we can sit on the dock and soak up the evening. With our brains we should be able to find a solution to Pete's problems by morning."

Pete met them at the driveway. "I'm gonna replace the mattress and repaint the floor," he said, jerking his head toward the cabin with red window trim and yellow police tape. "I've had four cancellations for next week."

"Okay," Josh said, "we need to talk. I've got some ideas."

The crunch of tires on gravel interrupted him. Josh recognized the man who stepped out of the Otter Tail County Sheriff's car immediately. "Brandon! Brandon Johnson. How the hell are you?"

Brandon sauntered to the group. "I'd be a lot better if that food critic hadn't decided to die at Maple Beach." He gestured toward the picnic tables. "Can we sit down and talk, Pete?"

"Josh came to help me out," Pete said. "Whatever you have to say to me, I want Josh to hear."

Brandon shrugged. "I'm not here to arrest you, but I don't have good news either." They sat at the table, Josh straddling the bench.

"Pete," Brandon said, "James Broad was definitely poisoned." Pete groaned, hands clenched on the table edge.

"How can you be sure?" Josh asked.

"He died of an amitriptyline overdose. It's an anti-depressant, one of the older ones. Apparently a lot of people take it."

"So why don't you think it was an accident?"

"First," Brandon ticked points off on his fingers, "there were no pill bottles in his cabin. Second, his doctor said he didn't prescribe it for him, and his druggist checked the database and said he'd never filled a prescription for any and neither had anyone else in his area, and fourth, every one we talked to said that James Broad was a cup half full instead of half empty kind of guy. He took great joy in the world and in his job."

"I know he loved food," Pete said. "It was all he talked about.

"And the last reason we don't think he killed himself," Brandon waggled his thumb, "was that we found traces of amitriptyline in the dregs of the malt on his bedside table."

"Malt?" Pete said. "Where'd he get that?"

"Good question," Brandon said. "Has Mac started serving malts?"

"Nope." Pete grinned crookedly. "Says he's a specialist, and hamburgers and fries are his specialty."

"That's what I thought," Brandon said, "But I needed to check it out."

"Does that mean they can reopen the grill?" Josh asked.

The sheriff was shaking his head. "It's still poisoning. The man doesn't go out. People don't come to visit him. Whatever happened, happened here. Until we can prove differently, the grill stays closed. Sorry."

🍁   🍁   🍁

Brandon drove off and Pete turned back to his guests. He rubbed the worry lines on his forehead. "Okay, now I'm desperate. If we don't get the grill open, I won't be able to pay for the food that's rotting in the fridge. I'm going crazy. What do we do? Talk to me about your idea."

"First things first," Josh said. "You got any cream soda wasting away in your fridge?"

"Cream soda, root beer, sarsaparilla, and orange." He turned to Genevieve. "I recommend the root beer. It's the best in the world."

"Ah." Josh took a long swig. "Good stuff. They don't sell this in New York. Okay," he continued. "You usually close the day after Labor Day, right?"

Pete nodded. "Summer's over then."

"Well, what if you advertise a special fall season – this year only – see the leaves, take advantage of the late season fishing, and as a Halloween bonus, stay at the haunted resort."

Pete choked on his root beer. Genevieve pounded her bottle on the table top. "Bates Motel," she crowed.

"Listen, Jenny," Pete began.

"Genevieve! Got it? My name is Genevieve. In grade school I bloodied Michael Dalton's nose for calling me Jenny." She waved her bottle in front of Pete's stunned face. "But I'll forgive you this time because you were right. This is great root beer."

"I can see it," she said to Josh. "Decorate the cabins for fall. Colored leaves, pumpkins, cornstalks. You could even make the interiors more, I don't know, 'at the lake.' You know, pines, moose, bear. Like they have in those cute lodges in New Hampshire."

Josh shook his head. "This isn't that kind of a resort, Genevieve."

" I noticed."

"No, I mean it. People come here year after year. They don't have to worry about kids or pets or mess. It's not like some fancy resorts where they don't want you to really relax, be yourself. Pete can't change things. Like the curtains in our cabin have been there since I was a kid. They make me feel good."

Pete cleared his throat. "Actually, they haven't been there that long. Mom bought a bolt of that cloth back in the sixties. She just kept making the same curtains over again when the old ones got too shabby." He turned to Genevieve. "Jill, my wife, says our decorating style is shabby chic. It seems to work for our customers."

Pete methodically scraped the label from his bottle with a fingernail. "Don't you think it would kill us to emphasize the death?"

"No worse than a murder." Josh said. "Does the Historical Society still have a haunted house at Halloween? It hasn't ruined their reputation. And with the grill open, at least weekends, you'd have some money coming in. We always wished you were open longer in the fall.

"We can piggy back your advertising with Leaf Days and Oktoberfest. Have weekly bonfires with old timers telling ghost stories." He looked at his old friend. "All these ideas are easy for me to come up with, but you'll have to actually do the work."

"Jay will be excited about the Halloween stuff. It's her favorite holiday. I guess, I guess we could try it."

"With that ringing endorsement," Genevieve said, "I'd like to bring us back to reality. None of that will help if one of you gets arrested for murder, or if the cops don't reopen the grill."

A howling gasp interrupted her, and a small tow headed girl dashed across the yard.

"Jay!" Josh called. "Don't I get a 'hello' hug?"

The girl shook her head violently and kept running.

"I don't know what's gotten into her. She didn't even come out to see you this morning. Ordinarily, she'd be hanging around, begging for your attention." Pete cocked his head, listening. "All right. The love of her life is coming for gas. I can hear his motor. Maybe she'll come out of hiding for him."

Pete and Josh started across the yard toward the gas dock. Genevieve trailed them. The sleek red boat nosed into the dock and it's driver vaulted out. Tall, tan, and muscular, his blonde hair drooped rakishly over a pair of mirrored sunglasses. Genevieve looked at his face and a memory stirred. He caught her glance and winked. "What do you think?" He gestured toward the boat, pride radiating off his body.

"What engine has she got?" Josh asked.

"Two standard supercharged 900 hp Mercury 900 SC V-8's. Want to see?"

Genevieve turned her back on the motor talk and crossed the street, trying to tease that flash of memory to the surface of her brain. She decided to explore the rest of the resort and started up the hill through the trees, toward a miniature version of a cabin, window trimmed in blue paint. She turned the corner of the building and realized it was a woodshed, piled almost to the roof with split logs. A cobweb shimmered in the door frame, and a chipmunk scolded her from the base of the pile. Genevieve hesitated, suddenly aware of the little sounds in the lake side quiet: a loon call, the chattering squirrels, and the soft muffled sob of a child.

"Jay?" Genevieve squatted, eyes searching the shadows in the shed for movement. "Do you know who I am?"

A sigh, then the girl spoke, voice barely above a whisper. "Daddy calls you the bitch from New York."

Genevieve straightened, surprised to feel hurt. "My name is Genevieve. I've been looking forward to meeting you. Josh says you're a great kid."

"I'm not great." Jay sobbed again. "Mr. Broad is dead and Uncle Mac's angry, and the grill is closed, and Daddy's sad, and Grandma's dying, and Mommy can't come home, and it's all my fault."

"Hey," Genevieve said. "Nobody could be in that much trouble. Come on out and we'll talk about it."

Jay sniffed. "I don't want anybody to find me."

"Can I come in?"

The girl's breath caught. "You won't tell the police where I am?"

"Promise."

"Okay, come on up."

"Up?" Genevieve raised her eyes to the roof, and saw the young girl crouched on the highest row of logs. "How did you get up there?"

"The logs are kind of like stairs, just be careful."

Slipping and cursing, Genevieve clambered up the wood pile. By the time she settled beside Jay, her knees were skinned, she had bark under her fingernails, and her hair hung in sweaty ringlets around her face. "This is a pretty good hiding place," Genevieve said, looking down toward the lake. All eight cabins were in view, each painted white with a different color window trim and matching colored metal lawn chairs. Two boats circled each other on the lake. A pair of geese with ten goslings swam parade style from dock to dock, the slight ripple of their wake spreading out behind them.

"Tell me about your Grandma," Genevieve said, looking down at the grubby little girl at her side. Jay's blonde braids were rapidly unbraiding themselves. Tears had left rivulets through the dirt on her face, and her ragged jeans didn't quite reach her ankles.

"Grandma Ellen," the child's voice hitched. "Mommy is taking care of Grandma Ellen and Uncle Mac says she's dying."

"You know what that means?" Genevieve asked.

"My turtle died. First it stopped moving and then it smelled bad and we buried it in the back yard." She looked up at Genevieve. "I heard Daddy say that Mr. Broad smelled bad too. Will that happen to Grandma Ellen?"

Genevieve touched the girl's hair, smoothing strands off her face. "Your Mom won't let that happen, I'm sure." She put her arm around the child's shoulders. "Why do you think it's your fault?"

Jay sighed again. "I don't really. But it is my fault Daddy's sad, and Uncle Mac's mad, and, and." She buried her face in her hands and her shoulders shook with sobs.

"Hush, hush," Genevieve pulled the girl onto her lap. "Your Daddy's sad because he's worried about the resort. And your Uncle Mac wants the grill open again. He's not mad at you." She wrapped Jay in her arms and rocked her. "It's not your fault."

Jay sobbed even harder. Then she turned to Genevieve and wrapped her arms around the woman's neck. "It is. It is my fault."

At a loss for what to say, Genevieve just continued to rock, until Jay's sobbing trailed off to sighs and sniffles again.

"I took the malt to Mr. Broad the night he died," Jay whispered.

"Oh," Genevieve breathed. "Why? Where did you get it? Your Uncle Mac doesn't make malts, does he?"

Jay shook her head. "If they arrest me for murder will Uncle Mac be able to open the grill again?"

"Oh Baby," Genevieve tightened her arms around the child. "Where did you get the malt? Who gave it to you?"

"My friend, Jeff," Jay whispered. "He came to see Mr. Broad before, and then he asked me to take the malt to Mr. Broad because he was in a hurry. He told me it was a surprise, like a pillow fairy present. But I got to be the pillow fairy.

"And Mr. Broad thanked me and was really happy and started drinking it right away. He didn't even use a straw. And now, and" Jay's voice broke, and the tears pooled at the base of her eyes spilled over. She ignored them, staring up at Genevieve. Her breath caught in a sob. "And now Mr. Broad's dead. And Uncle Mac's a good cook, so it must have been the malt."

"The malt your friend Jeff gave you?" Genevieve asked, her fury held tightly in control. Jay nodded. "What's his last name? Where does your friend Jeff live?"

Jay shrugged. "I only know him from here. We talk about fishing and boats and stuff. He has such a pretty red boat."

"Jeff is the man with the fast red boat?" Jay nodded. "The man who was just at the dock getting gas?" Jay nodded again.

Genevieve gave her a little shake. "You didn't do anything wrong. Do you believe me?"

Jay shook her head and then nodded.

"Okay. You go to your house and wash your face and brush your hair. I'm going to talk to your Daddy and Josh." She watched the little girl scramble down the wood pile, and followed more carefully. When Jay disappeared into her cabin, Genevieve walked down the hill to the picnic table.

"Hey Gwendolyn." Pete grinned at here when she sat down beside Josh. "Where have you been? You look like something the cat dragged in."

Genevieve ignored his teasing. "The guy in the cigarette boat. The pretty guy in the pretty boat. What's his name? What's he do? He looks so familiar to me."

"I don't know," Pete said. "Jeff something. He says he's in the hospitality trade, like me. But I don't think he likes the grill. Says it's not his kind of restaurant."

"Restaurant," Genevieve said, almost to herself. "Jeff. Jeff." Her eyes opened wide. "Jeff, the Silicon Chef. He did it!"

"Wha?" Pete asked. "What?" Josh said.

"He's Jeff Ferrel, better known as the Silicon Chef. He has a restaurant in Silicon Valley and James Broad panned it last month. Said the food was pedestrian." She grinned wildly at the men.

"How do you know this?" Josh asked.

"He was working on a book deal with Carrie, the editor in the office next door to mine. I've seen him there. Just didn't recognize him without a shirt on."

"Wow!" Pete said. "He's the first person I've heard of who might remotely even have had a reason to kill James Broad."

"He did it," Genevieve repeated. "He won't get a book contract if his restaurant is a failure."

"Right," Josh knocked her shoulder. "He came here from Silicon Valley in his cigarette boat to kill his nemesis James Broad the restaurant critic." He chuckled. "Just because you saw him in your office doesn't mean he killed his critic."

"No." Genevieve's smile was tight, her eyes bright with anger. "But he persuaded Jay to deliver a malt to James Broad the night Broad died. Jay saw him drink it."

"God damn him to hell!" Pete surged to his feet, fists clenched. "He used my daughter. I'll kill the guy myself."

"Wait, wait." Josh was on his feet too. ""Call Brandon. They'll catch him and then I'll help you kill him."

"No!" Genevieve over rode both male voices. "Pete, Jay's at your cabin. She really needs you to snuggle her, comfort her. Josh and I will talk to the cops."

"So," Brandon said to the group gathered round the green picnic table, "with Genevieve's I.D. of the man and Jay's story, we checked the drug database again. Ferrel got prescriptions from three different docs for amitriptyline starting the day after James Broad gave his restaurant the bad review. That was more than enough of the drug for a lethal dose. Guess it doesn't take much acting to sound depressed."

The moon was rising round and white over the hills by the time Brandon slid into his patrol car and drove off. The moonlight laid a glittering path on the lake straight to Maple Beach. On shore, warm yellow light streamed from the long front window of the grill. Mac was frying up five hamburgers and a family size order of fries. Pete cradled his daughter on his lap. She reached up to whisper in his ear and his face flushed.

"There is no way in the world we can thank you," he said. "Jay says I should apologize." He cleared his throat. "Genevieve, she's right. You're not a bitch."

Josh whooped. Genevieve nodded, a small smile on her lips. "Generally, I'm not. But I just might have seemed like one during the last twenty-four hours."

The grill door slammed and Mac carried six baskets to the table. "Any chance there's a veggie burger or a black bean burger in the lot?" Genevieve whispered to Josh.

"Nope." He grinned at her. "One hundred percent pasture fed beef. They're great! That's why James Broad, the great restaurant critic, spent three weeks here every summer, eating Mac's burgers."

"Yeah right," Genevieve muttered. Josh pushed a basket in front of her, opened a bottle of root beer for her and passed her the ketchup. She picked a fry from the huge basket of fries in the middle in the middle of the table. "Um, these are great." She ate another. And then she picked up the burger and bit into it. Tomato and mayonnaise squirted out the side of the burger and ran down the corner of her mouth. Genevieve closed her eyes and licked her lips. "Ummm." She opened her eyes to find four people watching her intently. She licked her lips again, and smiled. "This burger is to die for."

Hearing Polkas on the Plains

by Julia Meylor Simpson

I cannot explain why
I veer from Route 83
when the sign points left
to the boyhood home
of Lawrence Welk. A mile
or two of gravel and I end up
at a well-kept farm
on the banks of a large pond.

I cannot explain why
I get out of the car to take
photos of weathered signs,
a bandstand or a field
of wheat. Bird songs
and a soft whistle of wind
are the only music here.
It's just me in the audience.

I only know that something
tugs at me way out here,
back to Saturday nights
when we danced around
the living room linoleum

in pajamas and pin curls,
before we ever thought
we were too cool not to.

I Am as Old as Our Cabin

by Mary Satre Kerwin

I'd love to say that I remember when my grandfather, father and uncle put up the building that has lovingly been called "The Cabin" (and more recently referred to as "Valhalla") in the summer of 1956. I was in my first year, having debuted in October of 1955. Instead, I have the usual kaleidoscopic memories of early childhood visits to the beach, digging toes into warm sand and plastic shovels and buckets into the wet lapping of waves on the shore in the never-ending quest to construct an indestructible castle with a lake view. My father taught me to swim in Otter Tail Lake. I learned the fine points of telling fish stories from my grandfather, whose fame as a waffle maker was unmatched. I remember sharing quarters in early days with my Rundquist cousins before they made their move to Aunt Matilda's former cabin. Aunt Matilda was Aunt Clara's sister – Aunt Clara had the cabin next door to ours. It seemed in those days that most of the other folks in Camp were either related to us or had been to St. Olaf with my parents. Now that I think of it, things haven't changed that much.

My sisters and I used a "short cut" in the early days to gain access to friends living in the other cabins. Instead of going down our hill and taking the camp road, as is proper today, we would walk across the top of the hill, cutting through small clearings etched into the woods in the spaces between the cabins. In this manner I encountered Dr. Jacob Tanner, sometimes called Grandpa Tanner, at work at the table in his cabin. We did have the manners to pass quietly along this path so as not to disturb our elders in their working or napping, but often Dr. Tanner would gesture in a friendly manner and call out greetings as I passed, alone or with a sister or two in tow. I now realize that I had the honor of meeting the only surviving original founding member of Camp Nidaros at that time.

We could walk as far as Aunt Marion's and Uncle Art's cabin before heading down the drive towards Otter Tail Lake. We never managed to take the short cut through to the original Soelberg place as very young children, having a morbid hereditary fear of poison ivy (the woods were thicker between Narums' and Soelbergs' places). In later childhood, however, my sister Kris and I made the acquaintance of our grandmother's cousin, Bren Hobart, who taught French at Kris's junior high school in Sioux City, Iowa. Kris and I studied French – that made Aunt Bren very cool to us. But what fully captivated us during our summers at the Lakes was her vast collection of library books which she was totally willing to share with us. We also lived in Sioux City from 1965 to 1975 and a prelude to every family trip to the Lakes was a visit to the Sioux City Public Library to provide our summer reading material (no TVs at the Cabin – can't even remember when we first got a telephone; we used to play Barbie dolls or cut out items of furniture from the Sears catalog and stick them on a paper bag "house" posted on the wall for elaborate paper doll games). But Aunt Bren seemed to have some magic insight into the psyche of a teenage girl and the books she arrived with were must-reads for Kris and me.

There was a playhouse behind Aunt Marion's cabin, and our cousin (technically second cousin once removed) Linda Larson would host games for us there, also, followed by an occasional sleepover at Aunt Marion's.

Music played its part in our summers, and we frequently found ourselves in front of the congregation in the "Church in the Woods" teamed up with young folks from the Tanner family – Mary Elizabeth Egdahl (a really good guitar player) and her brother Jim, my good friend Sarah Govig, or sometimes the Eid family – Marion, Marge and Karl from Hong Kong (so distant and exotic in those days) or longtime playmates Deborah Eid or Stephanie Hageman. There was another Tanner family with almost as many girls as ours, and when our time at the Lakes coincided, Connie, Kristy, Kathy and Mary were also good companions and fellow performers in church. At least the audiences were always friendly!

I remember how my dad, on sawhorses in our driveway in Stewartville, Minnesota in the early 1960's, constructed from plywood the first sailboat I had ever seen. It was blue and white and sealed with fiberglass (he worked very hard to make it as smooth as possible). The original sails were orange and white and made from a parachute from a surplus store. In this superb craft we all had our first sailing lessons, and it seemed that travel on the lakes was changed forever from that time; our only previous mode of water transport was the family fishing boat powered with the 5 ½ "seahorse power" Johnson motor on permanent loan from my uncle.

As a recent St. Olaf grad in the late 70's I once brought several of my close friends to the Cabin in the autumn to experience the change of colors and seasons. We had to fetch our water from Walker Lake and sleep near the fireplace to keep warm, but it was a wonderful experience for me, sharing my special place with special people. Somewhere, I still keep a photograph of myself surrounded by these friends, with my grandfather's old beat-up hat on my head and my guitar on my knee.

My grandfather passed away during one of the next summers at the Lakes – in the woods, surrounded by the nature he had loved, and discovered by a dear old family friend (Olaf Storaasli). I begged off work as an RN at Fairview Southdale Hospital to join my parents as we drove out to the cabin to bring my grandmother home with us, still realizing that "home" was always there at the cabin my grandfather had built for all of us so many years ago.

Time passes and lives follow different paths. I brought my own husband to the Cabin in the early days – literally – of our marriage in February, 1981. We spent our fleeting honeymoon at my Uncle Willy and Aunt Jane's cabin – it was insulated. Hans Ronhovde ("Old Bus Driver") across the road made sure the toilet was working and took delight in calling on us to make sure everything was there that we needed. My uncle and aunt had left lovely provisions in the fridge and my new husband impressed me with his wood-chopping abilities. We cross-country skied on the lakes, which is totally amazing if you have never tried it. When his advertising job offer came through mid-week from Chicago, we packed most of what we owned into my Honda Civic and drove to Chicago to set up our new home.

One often thinks of the things one gives up to have a marriage and a family, but in our case, and largely thanks to my husband's insistence, the Lakes and the Cabin remained the one constant in my life, though Bob was not always able to accompany me. And so my most special memories are of bringing my own children to the Cabin and introducing them not only to all available friends and relatives, but also to my idyllic childhood memories and the "Lakes Way of Life." From Wellington, New Zealand, Melbourne, Australia, Hong Kong, Danbury, UK or Yokohama, Japan over many years we made the Lakes our summer destination – me, Laura, Daniel and Ryan. The fish stories were turned over to a new generation – my dad teaching my younger son that "there is fishing and there is catching" and my brother-in-law passing hours in his boat with his nephew during which few, if any, words were spoken (well, what do you really need to say?). My children learned lake lore and pursued sports on water and on land, christening a family-acquired plot of land between our cabin and the Rundquists' on Otter Tail as "Andy's Field" in honor of my cousin Andy Rundquist. Many games of various national origins have been conducted with full complement of cousins present on Andy's Field! And a personal favorite tradition continues – the "Fairy Hunt." See me later if you want the true story of this time-honored pastime.

Sometimes there was a summer when we couldn't travel to Minnesota – or to the USA, for that matter. Seasons run a different course in NZ and Australia, and when we had to stay for school during the months of June, July and August, we would have to alter our travel plans and pay a Christmas visit to the US relatives. One July I was in our home in the North Shore area of Auckland, NZ, when an indescribable feeling of nostalgia overtook me. I picked up my phone, thinking that even if no one was there to answer me, I would be comforted by the knowledge that I was connected to a ringing phone in the Cabin I loved so much. I guess it wasn't as much of a long shot as I had imagined, and my grandmother answered the phone. We chatted for awhile, and then I asked her who was currently in Camp. She said that her brother Trygve and his wife Ruth were there. They spent time renting a cabin at Barky's for a week during the summer so Uncle Trig could get his fishing in. She also said that Bren and Mars were up from Sioux City. Hooray, some of my favorite people! I asked her to give them my best. She answered: "They're right here!" and in the background I heard well-loved familiar voices call out "Hi, Mary!" Imagine the lucky timing getting all five of them with one phone call! It is a memory I hold especially close to my heart…all of those wonderful folks have since left this world.

I recall a conversation at Aunt Bren's place a few years ago. Her daughter Barb was there and one of her grandsons. I had wandered over to pay my respects and started asking questions about "the old days" and reminding her to get her memories jotted down for the 100th Anniversary. She said: "You expect me to be there, do you?!" with her usual touch of humor. Well, you never know…She told us of driving up from Sioux City in the early days of Camp in the old Model T, so crowded with family and belongings that her brother had to take his chances riding on the outside of the car – fine as long as it didn't rain. And we are not talking about a simple four-hour trip on the Interstate from the Cities to the Lakes. This was a two-day journey and meant to last for the entire summer. This place meant that much to folks in those early days.

I guess Bren was right, sadly, but she is with us as much as my own grandparents and other well-loved friends and relations, including the great-grandparents and great-great-grandparents I never met, but whose desire to seek out a place for rest and refreshment inspired the gathering that endures to this day, on the shores of Lakes Otter Tail and Walker and throughout the world, living in the hearts and minds of all who have loved the Lakes.

Fifty

by Warren D. Woessner

Pine sap in my hair,
sun in my face.
Steve joking, pointing out the peaks
above me on the ridge
I couldn't quite climb.
Still, the stream
far below my boots
is a bright ribbon
tying up the basin like a present
I can still open.
Chickadee and siskin have songs
not too high to hear,
and if I can't make it
all the way up,
I can still find a good way down.

February is Like This

by Laura L. Hansen

A good day of sun and snow melt
ice forming and re-forming on lakes and sidewalks and windshields
warmth that tempts us into lighter coats and long walks and imaginings
of daffodils
then this, this heavy snow skeining around light poles and plopping off
awnings
coating the toes of our boots

I take out the long scoop shovel
scraping white and grey stripes into the downtown sidewalk
curving off the edges as if making my own sacred (if clumsy) version of
crop circles
I see in the middle of the rolling furl of snow one crisp brown leaf
tumbling
like a dark sock in a load of whites

I wonder if the mallard I saw this morning angling awkwardly down
through the heavy sugar-coated sky was surprised by the sudden drop in
temperature overnight and by the hard blue sheen covering the last of the
waterholes
did he feel a panic rising up in his silent throat at the sight
of another spring slipping away

Winter Solstice

by Glorianne Swenson

Signing a six-month lease,
Winter took up residency in Minnesota.
Stealing days from autumn and spring,
She dug her frozen tentacles into the earth.

Spreading her icy canvas over prairie and plains,
She staked out her claim over vast arenas.
Her days were short and her nights were long;
Wrapping fields and frozen streams with snowy blankets.

The once naked trees now wore their
White robes in the frosty morning.
Their branches heavy with beauty,
But aching with the weight of winter cover.
Barely visible above white embankments,
The tall grass now brown and pale and blowing in the wind.
Reaching with outstretched arms for something;
Perhaps a ray of sun between etched gray December clouds.

Let this party be brief beneath the snowy skies,
But not before the children have made snow angels,
And old ones have warmed their bodies with hot cocoa and spiced cider.
Let them treasure the warmth by the fireplace before winter leaves.

Breaking Silence

by Gerri Stowman

From the third floor of the Otter Tail County Courthouse, I admire the building's mural-decorated rotunda and stained-glass dome. Minutes later, I walk into a large courtroom and sit down in the public gallery, two rows behind the county attorney's table.

A young woman enters and spots me. She jostles her slight body through the crowd and then stubs her shoe on the base of the pew-like bench in front of me. The echo reverberates, drawing attention from almost everyone in the room. Though she is tall, her ponytail and bare complexion peg her as a youth rather than a nursing student within days of graduation.

I worry others may think she's too young to sit through grim details of a sex-crime trial. "You should wear a little make-up," I whisper after she sits down. "You'd look older."

"I've been working at the hospital since six o'clock this morning!"

"But, you look about fifteen."

Like an impish child, she wrinkles her nose and replies in a soft voice, "You worry too much about what people think!"

We attend the trial to support the plaintiff, a friend who was sexually abused by her pastor when he counseled her for chronic depression. The case draws widespread media attention and polarizes the community. Some support the law, commending the county attorney's office for prosecuting the case. Others oppose the law, charging that the county is overzealous in its pursuit of justice.

When proceedings begin, the county attorney addresses the jury: "She sought counseling from him because he was her pastor, and her Christian faith was important to her, and she wanted Christian counseling."

Then, he says, her pastor sexualized the counseling relationship, and told her she was getting better: "She would call him on a regular basis for help and advice, and he would ask, 'What would you do without me?' And it kept getting, in her mind, worse and worse, and yet, she had promised to trust him."

When the plaintiff takes the witness stand, the nursing student presses a handful of tissues into my palm. She knows that, years earlier, a pastor who counseled me for depression urged me to divorce my husband, leave my family, and marry him. Though I escaped his advances, I didn't talk about the abuse for nearly two decades.

After sitting through five days of testimony, we return to the courthouse for the jury's decision. The judge warns observers to refrain from making public exclamations when the decision is announced, and then signals the bailiff to bring in the jury.

"Mr. Foreperson, has the jury reached a verdict?"

"We have, your honor."

The judge reaches for the paper, unfolds it, and reads aloud, "We, the jury, find the defendant guilty of criminal sexual conduct…"

Despite the judge's warning, some of the spectators gasp. A woman sitting behind the defense counsel complains, "But she said she consented!"

The nursing student turns toward me. "It's illegal for doctors to sexually abuse their patients," she whispers. "Consent isn't a defense! Do they think it should be different for pastors?"

The next day, The Forum newspaper in Fargo reports the conviction and prints an interview with another survivor and me about clergy abuse of adults. I show the front-page article to the nursing student and explain, "We have to talk openly about this! People should know that counselors who make romantic or sexual moves on people under their care are manipulating their trust—and breaking the law."

"I'm glad you're speaking out," she says. "It's easier for you to tell your story because you got away."

"I was only in counseling for six months when my pastor made his advances—it's harder to escape from someone who's been helping you for years."

When the nurse moves to Fargo-Moorhead, she says the criminal case in Otter Tail County changed her life: "I want to become a social worker and, someday, a counselor. And I want to help Christians understand this kind of abuse."

Now, eight years later, she holds a Master of Social Work degree, works in the Twin Cities, and advocates for abuse prevention in her inner-city church. I write about clergy abuse of adults and correspond with survivors who contact me through an organization offering free resources.

I ask. "Do you remember how worried I was when The Forum asked me to go public?"

"Yes," she says. "And I remember the anonymous letters you got after the article was published."

"You said I should do what God asks me to do and let Him take care of the rest."

"I'm glad you spoke out!"

"I didn't have a choice. Even though it happened a long time ago, it still hurts me, sometimes."

She looks puzzled. "After all these years? Why?"

I put my arm around her and meet her eyes. "You were only a baby when I entered counseling with our pastor. Following his advice would have wrecked my marriage and destroyed our family."

She hugs me.

I weep.

[Author's note: Trial quotations are from May 2, 2001, Volume II, State of Minnesota vs. defendant (trial transcript), Seventh Judicial District, County of Otter Tail.]

Giiwe: go home

by Christine Stark

I lost twenty-nine drawings and paintings when someone set fire to the turn-of-the-century two-story brick building on Cedar and 16th in south Minneapolis on January 17th, 2004. Whoever did it started the fire on the second floor and burned it down into the gallery. Three weeks after the fire my mother died from complications after fourteen months of chemotherapy. She was one treatment away from remission. I thought I had finally found my way home after winding across the country for years (Minnesota to Wisconsin to Minnesota to Oregon to Florida to Minnesota), but the fire and the death of my mother inched me further up the spine of Minnesota, until I landed a few hours from the Canadian border in the northwestern corner, perched on the lip of North Dakota, five minutes off the White Earth reservation.

I've come home, or so I've been told. The manidoog want me here, in this whitewashed expanse of drifting blowing snow and farm land clear cut by the Norwegian, German, and Swedish immigrants and their mixed blood offspring 125 years ago. Part white, part Anishinaabe, they and the full blood Europeans reversed the millennia growth of the forest in a few decades. The mixed bloods removed the home of their Indian ancestors so that the Europeans would have one. It was a true borderland life, constantly negotiating cultures from all over the world that landed on that particular spot of earth at that particular time in history to establish something called America. To create—out of anger, hatred, expediency, greed, and sometimes love—people who carry two opposing cultures in their skin. People like me.

After years of arguing with myself and various friends over whether I had any right to be part of Indian communities (I said I did not, my friends said I did), I finally made the leap and organized an art show and discussion series about sexual violence and African American and American Indian women. It consisted mostly of my work, over forty drawings and paintings, along with the healing masks of Samantha Emery, Native American dolls created by my friend Sherri, and the work of women from Breaking Free, an Afro-centric organization that helps women recover from sexual and physical violence. At the time, I was facilitating an art group at Breaking Free, and the women had made splendid masks of their faces out of plaster and bright paint to evoke the pain, trauma, and hope of their lives. Working with the Minnesota Indian Women's Sexual Assault Coalition, I'd scheduled a series of talks to address violence against Native American and African American women. I wanted to get to the heart of it: genocide and slavery.

The morning after the first meeting—a panel that addressed the history of Native American and African American women's sexual violence, healing, and activism—our arson flicked his Bic and turned our art and a one-hundred-year old building into smoke and ice-encrusted rubble. While the building burned, I stood in a crowd across the street, wincing as the firefighters sprayed arcs of water into the building, which then sheeted down the interior walls and drenched the art that had escaped the flames. A woman standing on the sidewalk next to me said There's always trouble on this corner and nodded toward the cemetery next to the building. Car accidents. Shootings. Fights. Drugs. Others nodded knowingly.

The southwest section of the gallery was less damaged and, despite being told not to by the fire chief, I surreptitiously slid my way through the slush covered street, inching closer and closer to the section where my newest pieces clung to the brick walls, knocked sideways by the force of the water and reverberations of the falling brick above. Some of them looked perfectly fine despite the carnage around them, their faces gleaming through the gray and icy day, while others looked soggy, yet alive.

I talked up two firemen standing next to me, their arms folded across their chests and their oversized tan canvas suits, as they waited for orders. Much to my surprise they waded across the blocked off street through the front door, into the less damaged part of the gallery, and grabbed twelve of my newest pieces—the ones that dealt with my intense and often painful feelings of having European, Anishinaabe, and Cherokee ancestry. They, too, had orders from the fire chief that no one was to enter the building for any reason. When they returned with my art I scribbled my home phone number on a scrap of paper in case they caught hell for entering the building and needed me to come to their defense. I took one last look at the smoldering inferno and then loaded my soggy art into the cab of my black Ford Ranger and headed home to north Minneapolis.

The fire and the death of my mother did not drive me out of Minneapolis, but they did set my final move toward home in motion. Since I left my parents' place at nineteen, I'd moved one to two times every year for nine years inside the city limits of Madison, Wisconsin. I eventually moved back to the Twin Cities, then decided that I needed to leave home in order to find home, so I headed to the west coast with my partner.

When I lived in Portland, Oregon I felt lost, alien to the temperate climate, gray drizzle, distant mountains, and the heavy mustiness that pervaded everything, especially the stacks at Powell's Bookstore where I worked. I did not like being two to three hours behind the rest of the country. I did not like the people. They struck me as rude, exclusive, and too hip for their own—or anyone else's—good. Some difficulties at my partner's work were all we needed to set off across the country, our puppy sick with giardia in the passenger's seat of the U Haul and me following in my red 92 Mazda hatchback with two foaming cats draped over the seats like fur stoles. We rumbled through Oregon and Idaho. In Utah, at a McDonald's parking lot, we scrambled to put our puppy and cats in their respective vehicles when two cowboys sauntered toward our assemblage. We figured they saw the rainbow sticker. I imagined a beating, our animals hurt. Nice to see some family round here, one of them said and tipped his hat. We set down the animals' cages and talked.

If I felt lost in Oregon, I was sunk in Florida. There it became apparent to me that I could not know myself if I was off the land I belonged to. I physically and spiritually yearned for Minnesota. I missed the woods, the lakes, the four seasons, the cold and snow, and the smell of freshwater lakes. I missed the foliage of Minnesota—high brush cranberries, sumac, towering pale purple lilac bushes, rhubarb, and white pines tall as four-story buildings. I did not like the fire ants, the sultry heat, the downpour that blasted Orlando for half an hour every afternoon at two, and the threat of alligators consuming my puppy in one gulp at virtually any watering hole. Bright blue and green peacocks scratched across rooftops and cabbage-like palm leaves waved beneath a cloudless sky. It was surreal. I was living in a foreign land. I would have moved back to Minnesota after one month, but we could not break our nine-month lease at the apartment complex. So I suffered the heat and the ants and the alligators, carrying my puppy up and down the outdoor black metal mesh staircase which he refused to stand on, terrified because he could see the ground beneath his paws.

I returned to Minnesota, driving through an Iowa snowstorm with my dog and a few belongings to my mother's house in Bloomington. After a week-long search for an affordable apartment that accepted animals, I flew back to Orlando and drove our entire household over the Tennessee mountains and through the blue hills of Kentucky to our 70s chalet-style drug dealer infested apartment in St. Paul. We were fortunate, though, to find a place at all. The housing market was tight—less than 1% vacancy because, according to friends of mine, the powers-that-be were interested in keeping out low income folks, particularly black people from Illinois who supposedly move to Minnesota to take advantage of the welfare system.

I had been trying to find home since I was six when we moved from a small lake in northern Minnesota to a suburb of Minneapolis. On the lake, we lived in a 400 square foot house half way between Aitkin (population 1,000) and Garrison (population 202). Even though there was an extreme amount of violence in my family, when I lived up north I knew something about myself. I belonged somewhere—to the woods and the lake and the trees. My friends were the Peking and mallard ducks, my collie puppy, and the neighbor's tawny cat. I caught sunnies off our dock and collected them in a steel bucket. I talked to them as they swam circles, fed them chunks of white bread, and then dumped them all back into the lake. I played in the mass of bright orange poppies as tall as I. I listened to the bobcat howl on the frozen lake at night, entranced yet fearful that it would eat Rascal, my puppy, who lived next to the garage in a hay and snow-packed igloo. There weren't many other children (or adults) in the area and I spent most of my time by myself. But I was not lonely.

When I was a child the wilderness was my home, while the house I lived in was something to escape. My mother and I survived my father and his friends' beatings, rapes, and verbal assaults in a variety of wood and plaster structures throughout rural and suburban Minnesota, but we never really had a home—a place of safety and refuge. Oddly enough, I have been obsessed with owning a house since I was nineteen years old, one with a yard to grow a garden and sit out in while the sun set. I think I was interested in buying a house because once I got away from my father, I realized I could live in a way that I had never known growing up. A house became symbolic of a home, of knowing who I was, belonging somewhere, having roots.

I spent my 20s in poverty and the thought of ever owning a home seemed unattainable. Living on the verge of homelessness was my reality and actually becoming homeless was a much more likely event than making payments on a Tudor. But in St. Paul I left poverty by working as a massage therapist at Juut Salon. My dream became a full-blown obsession, as much based on the fear of being out in the streets as it was based on the hopes of belonging somewhere. I decided even though I couldn't buy a house at that time, I could get one on a contract-for-deed until I was able to buy it outright. I searched the metropolitan newspapers, found one, and moved into a miniature one-bedroom pea green house in north Minneapolis. The yard was mud. A person could barely stand in the bathroom. There was a dealer and two pit bulls across the street. But there was a detached garage, no one from another apartment snoring on the floor above, and the Theo Wirth Parkway was two blocks away—a good place to run the dog and find the land inside the city.

I thought I'd found a home. But I was wrong. My partner and I were splitting apart, the house was miniscule and over-priced by about $40,000. My mother lent me some cash she came into from the sale of her house, I found a realtor and a broker who were willing to work with my abysmal credit and moved one mile south to a slightly larger house with a fenced-in grass yard that I bought for $60,000 less. It was one of the cheapest houses in all of the Twin Cities. It was trashed, smelled like a barn, and had cobwebs the size of my head. A small lake formed in the basement when it rained. Two inches of dust blanketed the woodwork and the tops of the pictures they left on the walls. Even my dog was disgusted by the dust. The first time I pulled down the previous tenants' yellowed lace curtains he jumped on them enthusiastically, but stopped immediately when dust billowed out, causing us both to sneeze repeatedly. He let me carry them out alone after that.

But the house was mine. After fourteen years of searching, I'd bought a house in my hometown. I expected I would live there for the rest of my life. The land, city, and people were familiar, there was a writing and art scene that was second only to New York, and there was cold and lots of snow.

For two years I worked part-time as a massage therapist, cleaned and remodeled the house, accompanied my mother to her chemotherapy treatments, and attended graduate school 1 ½ hours south of the cities. Then my relationship ended, my dog was almost nabbed one night from the back yard, my art burned, and my mother died. My home wasn't safe any longer. I was a mess—devastated, depressed, and lonely.

The night after my art burned I had a dream. A blackened, charred man stepped out of the still-smoldering carcass of a building on Cedar and 16th. He lurched toward me, a blue light flashing like a siren atop his head, then veered off to the right and disappeared into the crowd. In the dream, I felt he was looking for me. I feared that as he lunged about he would see me. Accidentally run into me. Grab me and drag me down, back into the building from which he'd escaped. But he didn't. He disappeared and I was left with dread, sweating in the dark in my house, fervently wishing an

Indian woman would call. I flicked on all my lights, sat in bed with my cats and dog, electrified by terror. It was one in the morning. The phone rang. It was my friend, Sam, from the art show. She said she had a feeling she should call me. She is eagle clan. I told her what happened. She cried, said I'd better get up there right away.

"Up there" was the White Earth reservation, where Sam lived, healing from years of sexual violence, homelessness, and the negation of being adopted by a Greek family when she was young and then raised as a Greek girl. She didn't know she was Anishinaabe until she was 27 years old. I had plans to visit her in a few months, after things settled down with my mother's death. I would see an Indian doctor, get my Indian name, and watch TV with Sam until three in the morning. But she said to get up there right away and so I did.

The next weekend my dog and I trundled up Interstate 94 over slick black ice roads. Around St. Cloud it began to snow. A bit farther north it became a white-out and the roads closed. I kept driving, weaving between the Road Closed signs posted on the heavy metal gates that the State Troopers dragged across the highways. I ignored the advice of a Super Motel 8 employee who told me to wait it out at her hotel, used the bathroom and dashed out the front door. I was headed toward something; I was driving away from something. I had to get to Sam's. Blizzard or no blizzard.

I have Indian ancestry on both sides of my family. One of my great-grandfathers was Cherokee and another was Anishinaabe. I was not raised with anything traditional, and my grandmothers rarely talked about being part Indian. They were fearful and unsure. They were ashamed. The most my family would say was "Yeah. We're part Cherokee. Pass the butter." No one said much else about it. The result was that virtually all ties in my family to being Indian were severed and no one knew what to do or think about it, so most of us ignored it.

Except me. When I was four, in the woods of northern Minnesota, I wanted to run away, find the Indians and live with them. I remember being young, settled into the deep back seats of cars when Cher's song about the Cherokee would slide out the speakers. If there was no one in the back seat with me, I would silently cry. If there was someone, I would fight back the tears, sadness welling up inside me as deep and as long as Mille Lacs Lake, the enormous waterway that nips Garrison on the lake's north side and runs along an Anishinaabe reservation on the west side.

Later, when we moved to a suburb of Minneapolis, I would stand between two bathroom mirrors to catch my profile. What I saw— flat cheeks, round face, and full lips— was startling and I would quickly turn away as if I had flashed a card in a poker game that I was supposed to keep hidden. I am light skinned, but nonetheless I had those experiences, that awareness, as a child. In my bones, or maybe my DNA, I knew I was different from the other girls in the suburb—those blond, blue eyed, pointy-faced girls who cared about things I didn't understand and didn't care about the things I understood.

I couldn't see more than ten feet in front of me; the snow pelted my windshield and clouded my headlights. My dog was seat belted in the jump seat. No one knew where I was; I had no cell phone; I could have gone off the road at any moment. No one was traveling, not even the cops. But the time had come to find out if I could be Indian. I had been hiding those feelings, that profile, that identity all of my life. I'd spent the previous four years arguing over whether I had any right to be Indian. The time had come to find out if there was another reason—beside the abuse— why I was never at home in my skin.

I went into the ditch once, but my four wheel drive pulled me out, so I drove slower and paid closer attention to the drifting mounds of snow on the road. Then the snow slowed to a simmer, and I could see around me. A few dark silhouettes of trees, an occasional silo and mammoth barn against the swirling charcoal gray sky. About forty-five minutes from Mahnomen, where Sam lived, I saw a familiar blue haze flash through the grayness. I caught my breath. It was the same light I'd seen on the charred man from my dream.

Sam greeted me at her door, a bowl of buffalo mac in one hand and a pearly blue and green abalone shell in the other. She burned sage and cedar. My dog curled up on one of her blankets and I relaxed on the couch. Just being in her apartment, the smell of the smudge and the food, put me at ease, reminded me of a home I'd never known, but had traveled many roads to find.

The next evening Sam and I headed out for Earl and Kathy's house. Sam is blind in one eye and I had never been to White Earth. On White Earth you can drive for hours and never pass a convenience store or gas station. The only light is from the stars and moon. We took a right instead of a left and became lost on the rural roads, arriving two hours after we told them we would. We had to stop three times, asking for Earl and Kathy's until we found a family who knew them and gave us directions. Earl and Kathy, being on Indian time, did not seem to mind our tardiness, and welcomed us into their home in Naytauwash. Kathy set down cups of black coffee while Earl fried up pancakes. Sam had told me in the car to say "bungee," which means "a little," when Earl offered me food or I would have a stack of pancakes high as the ceiling on my plate. It would be rude if I didn't eat what he gave me.

The four of us sat at their table in the kitchen and ate. I passed Earl some asema, told him I needed help. Sam made conversation about a variety of things unrelated to me and our visit, while I did my best to eat. The fire had set off terror from my childhood—old feelings of being told not to tell and the subsequent threats that if I did I would be hurt were on the loose. I couldn't contain them anymore. The night before I'd had a dream that my father and other men were chasing me through the woods. I ran, dodging tree trunks thick as my waist, swiping at undergrowth with my hands. They were just about to grab me when I plunged out of the woods and saw a chasm. I kept running, didn't stop to think, and flew over the chasm which I knew, at that time in my dream, my father and his men were not allowed to cross. While I was in the air, I turned and I laughed at them. They shot at me. I landed on the other side, the Indian side, and set off into the woods. The dream had a good ending. It was defiant. I escaped. But it was unsettling, too, as precursors of great change always are.

Kathy was quiet, sipping her coffee. Sam talked on. Earl laughed and occasionally said, "Oh" and "Ah hah" in his lilting Anishinaabe accent. I said nothing, hunched in a chair across from Kathy, the refrigerator behind me and the stove with a cast iron frying pan cooling to my left. Fourteen months of my mother's cancer. The fire. My life-long feeling of not belonging anywhere. The years of rape and battery and the stress of the unknown about the ceremony I was about to go through. What would Earl say? What would he do? What would happen in ceremony? I was there to get my Indian name, that's all I knew. All those feelings surfaced, bubbled, burst out.

My thoughts heaved. I did not belong. I did belong. Maybe I could get help, real help, not band-aid therapy. I could not get help. I was "unhelpable." I was Indian. I was not Indian. I was self-conscious, terrified, jumpy. I was out in the middle of the woods—five hours and one snow storm away from Minneapolis. I did not know Kathy and Earl, I was nearly crying, I needed help more than anything. My feelings and thoughts swung like a kids' carousel. Run. Stay. Up. Down. Belong. Don't belong. Round and round.

At some point I knew Earl was waiting for me to do something. I imagined thanking each of them individually and the second I thanked Earl, the last one, he stood up and said, "We're ready." I followed them, one of Sam's skirts pulled up over my ragged jeans, through the living room, down a short hall into a bedroom they used for ceremony.

I cannot write about what happened in the ceremony, but suffice it to say I was nervous. I trembled throughout it. Ceremony is raw, intense, beautiful, and powerful beyond words. It reaches inside you, connecting parts of yourself you never knew existed with the land, trees, water, stones, and all of life. It connects you with your ancestors and their way of life before the Europeans came. It connects you with a vibrant, contemporary Anishinaabe life. I barely breathed, all I wanted was to make it through the ceremony without screwing it up. I did, Earl gave me my Indian name, and Sam and I drove through the dark woods to her apartment.

Three weeks later my mother's bowel became blocked and she died unexpectedly. I went back to White Earth for more ceremonies, more healing, more belonging, more connecting. That summer I worked part-time and spent the rest of my free time up north, making new friends, helping with Defeat Diabetes Day at the Anishinaabe Center, and dancing in the White Earth powwow. On my way home from the powwow my car quit right outside of Detroit Lakes. I sat back and said, "Okay, manidoog, what now?" I ended up at an acquaintance's house where I spent the next several days waiting for my car. I moved near White Earth a few months later.

However, I still struggled with my identity. When I was on White Earth, with other Indian people, I felt Indian. When I was at school or work or just in the city in general I did not feel Indian. I felt like a poser. I struggled with the color of my skin, even though many of the Indians on White Earth can pass for white. I struggled with not growing up knowing anything about Anishinaabe or Cherokee ways and with my family's confusion. I struggled with white people who think returning to Indian ways is a joke, especially if you're light-skinned. But I never got those attitudes from other Indian people. They accepted me, welcomed me into their community. I danced and feasted and talked alongside Indians with blond hair, brown hair, red hair, and black hair dark and shiny as a crow's wing. My experience, at White Earth and at other Indian gatherings, is that most Indians accept the reality of an Indian Diaspora.

I lived in a small town that was once the border dividing the Anishinaabeg and the Dakota, a border created by white men to keep the Indians from quarrelling with each other and disrupting white settlers. The land around our home is at once beautiful and devastating. The patches of dense woods are stunning, teeming with life, thick with manidoog, but much of the woods are now gone. In their place is stripped farmland where once the Anishinaabeg and animals of all sizes hunted and birthed and played and died.

I learned more about Indian ways. I sat on porches and listened to how difficult it was for my grandmothers' generation to be Indian. How Indians lost housing, land, and jobs just for being Indian. Back then it didn't matter what your skin color was, if you were light-skinned and someone found out you were Indian you could lose everything—your house, your job, your children. You could be raped and beaten. I listened to Cherokee friends talk about how Cherokees had to instruct their children not to tell anyone they were Indian because white people could take their land. I listened to how Indians often passed as white, French, or Italian to protect themselves and their families. I listened to how the government and Christian churches destroyed connections to traditional culture by assimilation, theft of land, boarding schools, and outlawing of Indian religions. I listened to how Anishinaabe people had to go deep into the bush in order to keep traditional religion alive. How the U.S. government, which gives so much lip service to freedom, outlawed Indian religions until 1978. How all Indians did not get the vote until 1924.

I also learned how to sew blankets using four inch squares, how to feast the manidoog, how to do a four directions smudge, and how to cook traditional foods. And most importantly, I learned how to respect all of life and give thanks, everyday, for all life around me and my life. The more I learn about Anishinaabe ways, the more I understand that no matter what the white world says, I am Indian, inside and out.

Giiwe, I imagine my Anishinaabe ancestors saying as they watched over me all these years. Giiwe, I imagine them saying as I made yet another move to a different apartment, a different house, a different city, a different state. But I finally figured it out. I have found home inside and out. My ancestors are pleased.

Last Night in Mississippi

by Athena Kildegaard

Along this vining creek
crickets vie for wavelengths, my friend
has gone inside to her almost teenager
budding in the night, and I stand
a totem of silence, of having-gone.
Back for a visit I've been afraid to say
anything, it might come out all twisted
like a kerchief knotted twice too much.
It's been raining all day. Grass cowers,
magnolia blooms brim to collapse.
She's gone inside to her dishwasher
and the dog that needs a bath, to her
husband quiet as porcelain. I stand
where I can hear the loblollies creak
and complain, the wind shake down
the white oaks. It's all a crime.
That we cannot stay in one place.
That we cannot leave when we should,
because we're afraid or we're slow
with ourselves. I stand here
in the muggy night trying to hold
onto it, in case I don't return.
The blue hydrangea droops. Already
I'm forgetting the things I meant to say.

Divided By Eleven

by Conrad Røyksund

When I Was Eleven

I was eleven, when last I saw Henrik Olson
Little Grandpa
Smaller like Little Grandma
Than the next generation that followed them

I was eleven, when last anyone saw Henrik Olson
Because he died in his bed in the little house
Behind the big house
Not very big, either

I see him only at the corner of my eye
I was eleven
And nothing remains of what I saw then
Plainly, because of years

As when someone came to say
So I should not understand
That Little Grandpa was in his bed
Ever so quietly

When he was eighty-six

In from the corner of my eye
I see two things
That have never faded

Henrik and Anna walking
From the little house to the big one
Talking together about something I did not know
And could not understand
With words they had carried
From Norway

When they came with their daughter Olina
And her daughter Magna
To make a sand and peat life
In the woods of Washington

And Henrik, in the summer
On the long peat field
Across the ditch they had dug
To drain the swamp
And plant oats

Shocking hay
For the men who would pitch it
Onto the steel-wheeled horse-drawn wagon

Younger men than Henrik
Larger men than Little Grandpa
Who would pitch the loose hay
To be hauled like brown lace
Behind the team

I do not know if I carry Henrik's genes
But I carry two bright pictures
On the path and in the field
Before he lay down
With the words he had carried
From Norway

When I was eleven

When I Was Twenty-two

When I was twenty-two, burdened
With the birdshot of a liberal arts education

Scarred from having been used for target practice
By my Greek teacher
Who saw in my ineptitude
The erosion of smiling certainty
If actually I went to a seminary

I went to a seminary

In Berkeley
To become what other people wanted me to be
Because I was twenty-two

Big Grandpa, who read scriptures
And prayed at the long kitchen table
Had taken me aside and asked if I did not wish
To become a lawyer instead of a priest

Even at twenty-two I knew
That if you have been born
At the side of a long road
There are only two ways to go
And I went to California
To learn bright salads and sweet certainties

Where, like Abraham,
I became the father of a small nation
And custodian of unbelievable truths

At twenty-two, I never knew
An eight-hundred mile road
Following question-marked turns
And persistent curiosity
Would branch like a freedom-tree

Eventually

And that I would turn east
To Chicago
To become what I wanted to be

Having learned bright salads
When I was twenty-two

When I Was Thirty-three

When I was thirty-three
The people who were twenty-two
Hauled Old Glory down
And said our government lied to us

That the war in Vietnam was a crime
And a shame and a god-damned lie

When I was thirty-three
Angry students locked the Dean outside the door
And read his Draft Board files
Poured blood on his complicity
And stuck flowers down militia gun barrels

They said we'd overcome
After the Selma March and Washington D.C.
When the troops came home again

Some died later of flower-shot wounds

Born innocent
And forced by evolution to know
That thinking is not an option
And that inheritance is not destiny

At thirty-three
Wanting something I remembered

Before we became a manifest destiny
I stood reluctantly
And wanted not to sing again

Bombs bursting in air
Liberty and justice for all
Our flag was not still there
At the dawn's early light

They lied and made us want to cry

They stole my innocence
When I was thirty-three
At the university

Chicago
Hog butcher for the world
Tool maker, stacker of wheat
Irish-Polish-All-American muscle
What had we become

I wanted to be free
Of innocence and trajectory

Wisdom came flowered
Smelling acidly of honesty
Grown-up children chained the doors
Marched across bridges, singing new songs

Killing fields and clubs and dogs
Racial hate and white crosses
Buses with back seats, and blindfolded buildups in Vietnam
Everything came smoking down
When I was thirty-three

I carried twice the books
To hold myself down
While honesty rose like flames
To burn the fingers of assumption

After a while

I carried my head gingerly
To a Wish-Doctor and asked him
To screw it on straight

Wishing none of this had happened
But knowing it had

I have lived cross-threaded ever since
I was thirty-three

When I Was Forty-Four

When I was forty-four
I sat at our dining room table
Where we met every evening
And talked about the day

Weaving our lives together
As they had been together
From California through Chicago
Until we reached the promised land
Where I had dragged them
Because my demon was stronger than theirs

I had gone from the collared priesthood
To dig a hole deeper into doubt
Than they knew or wanted

They trudged
California, Chicago, Tübingen, Chicago, Decorah
Reluctantly or innocently

We sat at the dining room table
And I tremble-voice told them that it was like this
That I was like the pepper shaker
And their Mom was like the salt shaker

And I shook like the shakers

Starting in Tacoma and Toledo
Meeting in Berkeley
Where our trajectories had brought us
To the same place

And I curved the shakers in arcs
Talking about salt and pepper shakers
Side-by-side
Like a little bride and groom

Both true to where we had always been going
Our arcs continued on
Away from that meeting place

While they sat there uncomprehending
Of the demon that moved salt and pepper shakers
Across the dining room table

I held tight to the salt and pepper shakers
Because I did not know what to say about
The real people at the dining room table

Not knowing how to explain
How one goes from near to far
In what was not a betrayal but an arc
How their mother's life was as true as mine

Now the pepper shaker was here
And the salt shaker there

I wanted to cry at the rotten absurdity of it
At the pathetic shambles of it

Why am I asking our children to understand
What we do not understand

When I was forty-four
I wondered what had determined everything early
Driven us inexorably to where we were about to fall off
The edge of the table

One here, the other over there

Numb and dumb like salt and pepper shakers
We could not say
What we did not understand

I should not want to be forty-four
Ever
Or again

When I Was Fifty-five

We drove east on I-10 at my age
I was the national speed limit

Driving a new-to-us-Oklahoma-used pickup
Dragging a tired trailer from Tucson
Back to Iowa greenfields

Feeling good
Feeling new feeling used
Thinking back thinking next

Academic degrees we needed more than wanted
In hand
To go to where we had long-time been

Three years we had been students again
Credentialled for a new life in an old place
Remodeled to teach computer information systems

Because the Religion and Philosophy Department
Believed in believers
And the Dean believed we were a pair

We computer-coded a detour
Through to a new major
Of minor consequence

I should return with a stud in my nose

Mari said
And you with an earring

Instead I disguised myself by changing my name
To what Ellis Island had taken from my father
And wore cowboy boots

When I was fifty-five
We told Felix the Wonderdog that we were going for a ride
And he jumped up onto the seat and said Let's go
Nose to the passing air
His map

Content with the miles between
Excited only by Arizona and Iowa

We went back to where he had been born
Fifty-five dog years earlier
And watched him sit up nose up when we crossed the Missouri
To what smelled familiar and strange

Another old dog coming back

An dog with a nose full of desert dust
In a pickup held together with red Oklahoma dirt
To Northeast Iowa
Green and gray and familiar

Where friends were firmware
And policies hardware

Do you think he worry-asked one day
There is a chance
Luther will tenure a Methodist like me

You have to understand I said
When enrollment drops like this
They fear they've lost their roots and soul
And go to chapel singing hymns

Checking to see who isn't there

It is like a sine wave
Memorize A Mighty Fortress
For the dipping-down times

Felix and I crossed the river humming Wide Missouri
Into greengrass
Riding a sine wave
Doing fifty-five

When I Was Sixty-six

When I was sixty-six
One pants leg on
I told Mari it would be my last year to teach
Good she said Put on the other leg

Dawn-early
I told the Dean and his dog it would be my last year
Good he said while his dog stared away

This house is so big Mari said
Let us sell it and move on
The Dean said he would buy it
Good I said

Time to get even with his dog

We threw away most of what we owned
Moved all the heavy things to Tucson
Stored six tons more in seven places
And rented an apartment next to a tarantula

Desert rats
Starting over
When I was sixty-six

Marty said I could put my saw in his garage
So I cut two fingers off
Drove to the emergency room with my hand in a bag

The doctor sewed them back on

Old Timer Baseball came later
After my fingers stayed put
Stiff
My glove hand

What are you going to do when you retire
Everyone asks
I told them retirement isn't just golf
Or golf at all
If you have a saw

I left my wristwatch on the dresser until it died
Turned off the alarm clock
Started waking up to greet the sun
Lying down when it got dark

Tried to convince Mari that a crowing rooster
Would make a nice early Matins call

Have you gone mad she said
Take up Buddhism
Something quiet
Sleep in

Looking forward to the day
Wondering how to get it all done
Not caring if I didn't

Taking revenge on the industrial revolution
And marching in step
Measuring out lunchtimes

Stopped work whenever I damned well pleased
Early or late

Bought a house Painted it The neighbor's house too
Repaired the windows Finished the cabinets
Painted the pool Fixed the pump Coated the roof
Put in a circular driveway Hauled tons of rocks

Made flower beds Installed a water system
Fed javelinas Sweat Swore Built a new door

Retirement is not a job for old people

In Tucson now aren't you they asked in Iowa
Playing a lot of golf Keeping busy Have a hobby

Not a clue what people do
When they are sixty-six

Now That I Am Seventy-seven

Now that I am seventy-seven
The boat I built these last three years
Broods the winter days away

Glad for the roof and wondering at darkness
Innocent that Spring is half a year away

What will you do now my neighbors like to ask
Assuming that project-end is end-of-life
Idea is an only child

I want to say I will build a bridge over troubled waters
But I'd have to sell the boat to do that
Still be a little short
Take the boat instead

Now that I am seventy-seven
I am going to walk indoors more
Not so much to keep warm
As to keep from getting mugged in the morning dark

Minnesota Nice isn't always

Summer I will climb the corporate ladder
Up against the east wall
Scrape paint Paint paint
Bow my arches up

At seventy-seven I worry less about conformity
Time to let my thoughts run free
I think I'll say just what I think
Short of cruelty

Maybe buy a drover coat
Learn to swear
Properly
Nothing about crude intercourse
Insult the gods instead and all the angels too

Discard all my might-have-beens
Think about possibility

Locate the horizon
Plan my next eleven

While I am seventy-seven

Long Cold

By Bill Holm

After many days far below zero
your body forgets even its desire
for warmth, pleasure, love.
Is something naked under that armor?
You can't quite remember what.
You sigh, shiver, let it go at that.
Once, wind carried the world's smell:
Pig barns, cut grass, fried grease, apples.
Now it is odor-free, even the road kill
refuses to rot, becomes an ice boulder.
What's the good news here at the pole
of cold and inaccessibility? All
the death bacteria and biting insects
will wait awhile to do their work.
Unless you survive, they never arrive at all.
There's a reason for staying alive.

Acknowledgement

A special "Thanks" to the Lake Region Arts Council, whose grant funding made this project possible. For more information about the LRAC, or to make a donation, please contact them at: 133 South Mill Street, Fergus Falls, Minnesota, 56537; (218) 739-5780.